WALSH'S LAIR BOOK 4

KATHI S. BARTON

World Castle Publishing, LLC
Pensacola, Florida
Copyright © 2025 Kathi S. Barton
Hardback ISBN: 9798288311345
Paperback ISBN: 9798891264199
eBook ISBN: 9798891264205
First Edition World Castle Publishing, LLC, June 23, 2025
http://www.worldcastlepublishing.com
Licensing Notes
Cover: Cover Designs by Karen
Editor: Karen Fuller

Prologue

The Gathering Storm
~~The Peace of being without war~~
~~Evenness of mind, temper, and composure~~
~~Create by imagination, invention, and design~~

Storm walked around the little store listening to the gossip about one of the biggest disasters ever recorded — at least how these people were now witnessing it. She shook her head in amazement. How could humans be so insensitive? Not to mention stupid. That was one of the million and one reasons that she didn't hang out with humans for too long. They not only were, for the most part, clueless, but they seemed to have rose-colored glasses on all the time. The rumor mill was running full blast, it seemed today.

"They say that thousands of those bastards are dead. The whole place just split the roads and ate'em right up. Can't you just imagine what they were thinking when they were being swallowed up like that? I can't, I tell you what." The man behind the counter had himself a great audience, and he was taking full advantage of it today.

"Heard tell that them there houses just toppled over like the kid's blocks. Smashing people while they slept in their beds." The man speaking shook his head. "Mercy sakes alive. It sure did a nasty bit of business over there on that street."

"God is taking some sort of vengeance on them there foreigners. Sure as I'm a 'sitting here, it's God doing them people in." She actually had to physically close her own mouth when the person made that statement. "They should have stayed in their own place now here where we people are." Storm wondered if a one of the people standing at the counter knew that they were all foreigners to this land.

She also wondered what they'd say about her and her sister if they knew what they really were, which made her smile. She wasn't going to speculate on it too much, but they'd have plenty to say. There was no doubt about that. They couldn't have gotten more foreigners than they were.

Storm and her twin sister, Ember, were time adjusters for the world. They, like a great many other beings, moved throughout time and made slight adjustments in the fabric of reality when and where it was needed, smoothing out the lines so that it looked untouched, perfect. They'd been doing it longer than any of the beings in this room had been alive. And they would continue to do so long after they were nothing more than dust in their graves. Humans and shifters alike had no idea how many times they'd been recused from their own stupidity.

To do their jobs, they would travel back and forth, sliding into whatever persona was needed to blend into the world they were in. It took great strength and lots of practice to even attempt what they did for the world. Sometimes, they were the only ones standing between the extinction of mankind and the world being populated at any given time. Storm caught a reflection of her face as she walked around the little odds and ends store.

Tall, at just over six-foot, Storm was well-proportioned and athletic. Of course, no one would see that under her long dress and equally long sleeves. Her long dark hair, when not pulled into a tight bun at the back of her head as it was now, hung nearly to her waist in springy corkscrew ringlets. Her wings, too, pressed tightly against her back and legs only gave a small hint of what she really was.

Her skin, like her sisters, was alabaster and smooth as velvet. The only mark that marred their skin was the tattoo of their kind. It was a dragon that wore the wings that curled around their back and clawed hands, seemingly holding onto their shoulders while the tail trailed down their ribs and wrapped around their legs. Storms on her left leg, Embers to her right.

When their wings were spread and covering their arms from shoulders to their wrists, it would be, she supposed, frightening to anyone who would see her without any knowledge of what she was. Smiling at the men when they tipped their hats at her, she put her purchases on the counter and waited her turn to be waited on.

At the moment, Storm was in the year nineteen hundred and twenty-three in the body of a school teacher about to start "schooling" the area children in their reading, writing, and arithmetic. It was the closest body that fit her size when she popped into the time zone. The teacher would have no memories of her being Storm for a bit. There would be a slight accident, a small tumble that would alter her memories. Not that she'd remember Storm and what she had done, but the teacher would recover easily and never be the wiser of what she'd done for her world.

This time, working in this area, it had been a small fix. A mountain had come down on a family that was digging for clay and killed the youngest child. Storm had been tasked to save the child. Her future and that of a great many generations beyond her hadn't been born if she'd been killed. Saving the family, simply making them later than they had planned to the mountainside, had done the trick. The mom, always so organized, would forget to bring the cold water she'd stored in the creek that ran by their home to keep it nice and chilled for them all. Storm loved it when it was something like this had been.

There were times when whole realities had to be altered. Generations needed to be moved ahead to save someone. Sometimes, it was to save a being or one of the descendants of a human who was needed in the future. Other times, it was to erase a horrific time in the lives of humans — mostly, it was natural disasters where many deaths occurred. Humans, for the most part, would change up their entire lives, nothing to do with the ones that had been killed because they were witnesses to something so horrific that they had seen. It was all in the timing, she knew.

Other times, it was the consequences of the disaster that were too large and affected too many things when they rippled down through the ages and had to be removed. Something as simple as a house being crushed with their things inside. It could have been the witnessing of a family pet being killed. Any and all things that would alter everything, and it was up to them to repair the damage that had been done.

As Time Displacement Officers, they were there to ensure that the shifts were smooth, with no overlapping lines after the time frame was removed or fixed. Storm would watch an event, something that she'd fixed a thousand times to make sure that things were normal. However, gifted humans or small children saw the flaws. It was easily explained as déjà vu. Or a dream, too. Small children would complain to their mothers or fathers about how they'd done this before, only to be told that they were wrong. Poor little tykes. She would believe her children should she ever find herself a mate. Not that she was looking for one.

Storm was also there to capture another of their kind and bring him to justice. It was he who had moved the family to the mountain for the one to be killed. And he would have profited off of the disaster had she not been there when it unfolded. That neither was something that they could let happen. Everything you did, even from pulling a leaf off of a tree, would affect generations of families, she'd come to learn. And that was the very thing that the other being was doing — affecting generations of families for his own profit.

His name was Grail. He had been altering reality to suit his own personal gain and to profit for a while now, but no one could catch him. She was determined to find and make him pay before he could cause any more trouble. Altering a timeline too often would lead to sloppy work and time twitches that people would notice. And that was something that she was afraid of more than anything that she'd encountered in the human world. Too many glitches would wake the residents of the world to question what was going on, and it would — nearly all the time make them question their sanity.

Profit and notoriety from their jobs, both of which were laws that carried the sentence of death if broken, was what he had been doing today. Storm shuddered at the thought of the death he would endure when they took him back to Chilast, their magical realm. Death would not come easily or quickly for one like Grail. He had to know that. So why was he doing this when he knew it was only a matter of time before he was caught? No one knew the answer to that.

They didn't have the people to chase after him and keep the world and its people safe. As it was now, they were stretched to the limit. Working from sun up to sun down and all the between time too, it had been so long since she'd had a day off that she wanted to just lie down, pull some leaves over her, and got to sleep for about a thousand years.

Storm's twin sister, Ember, had gone to Tokyo to study and gather names of their kind for the continuation of their race. So far, all she'd been able to find was the list of dead. All of the dragons that had come after her and a few others who had been killed were on that list. That wasn't doing any of them a bit of good, and they all knew it. They were aging out, the lot of them, and there wasn't anything that they could do about it.

It didn't bother their kind when they would wind time backward. It was the moving of time forward that would harm them. Time, it would add, even if it was only a click of a second to their age. And having to look at something over and over, forward and back, it might well add as many as ten minutes onto their long lives. After a while and all those adding up, a dragon would age quicker, worn down by time and effort, because without rest and some time off, they'd just fade away like all the other creatures in the world.

Storm had been sent to the Americas for her assignment to find and collect Grail before he could act on his plan. If they didn't find him, and soon, all the work they'd kept up with would be useless. They'd all be dead, and there wasn't anything that could be done about it after that.

But she had a feeling this time was different. They knew his plan, what he had needed, and who to make himself in a new body to get away. It was what they had needed, what they were counting on to bring him to heel and to make all their lives safer without him in their worlds.

There was supposed to be a natural disaster, a large-scale shift in the earth's interior makeup that would cause the entire state of California to drift into the deep ocean and sink, killing all the inhabitants there. There were people there that he needed to complete the next phase of his power play against his own kind. She had been sent there to make sure that it didn't happen and to bring Grail to the Laws of the Realm.

Those people, men, and women alike, were the pioneers of the future that Grail was manipulating. Their collective knowledge would be passed down to their children and then on to the next generation. They were brilliant and would revolutionize the world with Grail's backing and help. And not in a good way that would only benefit themselves and no one else.

They, like Grail, were evil and only thought to gain untold riches and wealth from sources within the different timelines that he was supposed to care for. From future records, the Time Displacement Office – the TDO and the Elders of their kind, knew that he had taken this opportunity to steal them away along with all their equipment. In the aftermath of the devastating slide, everyone would assume they had been killed as well. After decades of exhaustive tracing and retracing the lines of time back, the TDO knew this was where he made his first move to bring his plan to fruition.

But the quake, the distraction as it was never to happen. At least not where it had happened in the history they had studied. It had happened the day before in Tokyo, where Ember was studying and gathering information. She worried for her, and when she couldn't contact her, she just knew the worst had happened.

Storm had been trying to contact her sister for hours without luck. They were both immortals and could shift and fly away if danger was imminent, but with the suddenness of the quake in Tokyo and the horrific scale on which it had occurred, Storm feared her sister needed her and needed her now.

Storm felt the first touches of Ember as she exited the store. The feelings got stronger the more Storm concentrated on her sister's touch to her mind. It was all she could do to keep an eye out as to where she was going and thinking about her sister at the same time.

"Are you all right? I've been trying to reach you for hours. What's happened?" Storm said as soon as the link was snapped into place between them. Ember told her that she was fine, never better. "I've been so worried about you that I can barely breathe."

"There are signs of him here. I have contacted several of our kind in the area, and they say that he stayed with them for one night two days ago. I can smell him and his poison here deep within the belly of the mountains where the records are kept." Storm smiled at her greeting. Ember was never one to mince words when it came to their jobs.

"Did he hurt any of them? Ask them for their help?" It would be just like him to murder them all just to throw them off his scent. But, at least for now, he only killed when he could gain from it.

"No. He spoke to no one but the people who were kind enough to allow him to rest at their dwellings. They say that he had a satchel with him, but he didn't seem to want to let anyone know what was in it. The Elders found a small thread, or we may not have known that he was even here. He's either getting better at hiding from us, or we're getting worse at our job, Storm."

"It's the same story here. He spent a night with the others here and then left. No one mentioned a satchel, though. He moved the place and altered the fabric where he had been. Ember, he didn't take the people he had before. Somehow, he has modified the events of that night yet again." Storm was suddenly terrified, and she was sure things were going to get worse before they caught up with him. "What do you suppose was in the sachet? I mean, is it important, you think?"

"Moran, the one who was closest to him when he was here, said that it had photos in it. Some of them were old tin types, others digital, and one hologram. He thought they looked like me, but the eyes were the wrong color. I'm assuming that it must have been of you. Also, from what I could gather, there were images of the people in California. There…there was a picture of a man, as well. One that we've not encountered in all our searches as yet."

"Photos? Maybe he's using outside help trying to find these people. Makes sense that he would have pictures. He'd have to show them who to look for, right? No, he didn't take anyone, as far as I can tell. It's…he's changed everything again."

There was a long pause through their connection; Storm could feel her sister's tension.

"What is it? Something has happened. Tell me."

"The Elders, they called to me two days ago. They needed an extraction. I…they had me take a human away from a deadly shooting. I've no details yet, but he is to be guarded at all costs. I have him deep within the mountains with us. He is curious but not frightened. I think that is why there was a shift in the location of where the quake happened. I think we missed this man somehow, and we angered Grail by taking him. He was in one of the photos in Grail's collection. Storm, this man, he was to die."

"Who is he? Had he been taken by Grail before? Is he one of Grail's minions?" She was more worried for her sister's safety than ever before.

"No. He isn't like that. His mind and body are pure. His spirit is clear. The shooting I took him from killed the others like him – men who uphold the law. I barely made it to him before the killings began in a house in New York. My wings were damaged slightly; I've been in a healing sleep until now." Still, Storm could feel her hesitation.

"Tell me the rest, Ember." She could have looked, she supposed, but in her current state, she knew that she'd hurt her sister. And she didn't want to do that. Hurting her would hurt her as well. "Ember?"

"I've been...the others here, we've...I've formed a bond with one. I've found my mate, Storm. After all this time, I've found my mate, and I'm afraid. Not of him, no, but what this is going to mean for the two of us. They will curtail my work soon."

Storm felt her heart stutter to a stop. Her mate, Ember had found her mate. Storm moved to the outer wall of the store and leaned heavily against it. This would change everything. Ember could no longer help her with their job. As soon as Storm thought it, she felt horrible. Ember had found her mate. She should be rejoicing.

"Storm, please don't be mad. I didn't mean for this to happen." She had hurt her anyway. The tone of Ember's voice told her that.

"Don't be ridiculous. I'm happy for you. It's just a surprise, that's all. I wish you nothing but happiness and good fortune. I love you." Storm, stronger now because she had heard from Ember and knew that her sister was going to be all right, continued. "I'm going to contact the Elders and see what they want me to do now. You'll be all right for now? You're making sure that you're all safe while you work?"

"Yes, I am fine. Thank you, Sister. I will be waiting for you in our cave. You let me know when you will be arriving, and I'll be watching the sky for you."

Storm hoped it would be that easy, but knowing the Elders as she did, she doubted it very much. They would want something from her, and she'd do it because Storm was loyal to a fault.

~~Devotion to the continued existence of life~~
~~Devotion to the supreme good~~
~~Pure condition of body and mind~~

It was against the Laws of the Realm to appear before the Elders in any other form than the one that you had been born to. She didn't mind that so much as she loved being a dragon whenever she could. As soon as Storm arrived at the castle, she reached out to touch the magistrate to set up a meeting with the Elders and the Queen. She was both surprised and terrified that they had readily agreed to see her as soon as she had eaten and shifted.

Food was brought to her, and she enjoyed a large meal. As soon as she had finished, she knew that she needed to complete her mission and get back to her sister. Moving to the outdoor paddock just outside her suite of rooms, Storm began her shift.

She loved to be a human. Storm loved the soft textures of their skin, the feel of the hair upon the body. She also loved the way the fingers bent and was able to grasp things within them. The light feelings of simply walking would make her giddy with anticipation of stepping into the grass or sand with her bare feet. But to be her true self, there was nothing better.

Storm was a dragon, an Enneahedral Dragon — also known as a Ninefold Dragon. She was as rare as any being could be. Storm was the ninth daughter of nine daughters for nine generations. When she had been hatched, she had inherited all the elementals of the earth and the nine directives as well. Her powers were nine times that of her sister Ember — even though she'd only been seconds behind her in coming out of her shell and abilities that went beyond any other dragons.

With being the ninth in so many lines, Storm was to be Queen of their kind as soon as she found a mate worthy of her and her love. But she was in no hurry to find either. She was too busy to care for a lover and didn't want one slowing her down either.

As soon as she stepped into the magical arena, she let her body respond to the pull of her Dragon. First, her body elongated, her spine curving and pulling, stretching to accommodate the large bulk of her form. Then her feet, dainty and small as a human, they too stretched, and great claws formed at the toes. The wings at her back began pulling away from her body and forming into a great expanse, wide and full. Flapping them once, she felt the blood surge through them, and then she pulled them tight against her body. Her face molded and formed into a massive head, teeth a foot in length and sharp as the talons at her feet filled her mouth full and lethal. The human skin along her arms became scales of great strength, able to protect her from any weapon, small or large. Her scales shimmered in the moonlight, catching and reflecting the gold and silver that blazed within each protective shell. By the time the shift was complete, Storm was a massive twenty-five feet tall, seventy feet wide with her wingspan, and weighed several tons of pure muscle and bone. She moved to the large door that went directly into the throne room and bowed before the other dragons gathered there, careful of every step that she took.

"Mistress Storm, thank you for coming to see us so quickly. We have much to discuss." Storm dipped her head to hide her confusion. They had expected her?

"You must go to China. We need for you to bring back the man Alexander Walsh. It is imperative that he survives. He is vital to the future of our race, to all of us."

"Pardon me, Sire, but my sister, Ember, she is —" Storm started to tell them what she was sure that they already knew, but they cut her off.

"Ember is going to have a hatchling soon. She must stay hidden. If Grail finds her, he will destroy her and the babe. No, it is you who needs to go and bring him back to us. May we count on you to serve us well, Mistress Storm?"

"Of course." Storm bowed before them and took a step back to leave the room. She was stopped by a slight cough from behind her.

"My lords, have you yet told the Mistress what is expected of her?" Storm startled. The being was small but by no means diminished in her stature. Standing before her was the strongest being anyone had ever known. Her mother, Queen of the Enneahedral Dragon clan, had swept into the room, her strength preceding her. "I will take it upon myself to do that now. You're dismissed." The people in the room disappeared at her command.

"Mother, you look well." Storm never knew how to speak to her mother, Morning. She had always intimidated her. Now was no different. Her beauty was one of the reasons. The other was that her mother wasn't really the affectionate sort of person. But then, neither was she.

"You look beautiful, child. I would like for you to shift and meet me in my private chamber. I should like to speak to you about this mission." Nodding once, her mother smiled. "We'll have a luncheon, you and I. And tea. I should like to speak to you about your other adventures, too, if you would allow it."

Immediately, Storm's body started its shift to human form. Within seconds, she was dressed similarly to her mother in a long silk robe with their crest blazing over their hearts. Storm nearly stepped back from her as Morning was standing very close. Surprisingly, Morning reached out and hugged her close to her.

The tightness of the hug had tears fill her eyes. It had been forever since her mother had hugged her, much less had hugged her first. Wrapping her arms around her mother, she heard her soft sob, and when she pulled away, her mother turned her back to her and started talking. As if nothing had happened.

"This man, Alex, you will bring him back to us safe. It's important." They were seated in the large room that her mother used when she came to the castle's offices. "I know that your sister is there, but she is breeding now. Thank the gods, and it's important to all of us that she be able to deliver her hatchling safely." Her mom sat down, so Storm did the same in an equally ornate chair.

It was not a question, but Storm answered her anyway. "Yes. You can trust me to keep him safe."

"It's not his safety that I worry about. It's yours." Morning shifted in her seat. An unease was evident on her face and posture. "Alex is your mate. It is determined by the Elders that he will father the next line. His bloodline is strong and pure. He will provide you with love and companionship for the rest of your life and on into the next. You and he and the family you breed will be the ones to destroy evil. "

Storm looked sharply at her mother. No. No, this could not be happening. She did not want a mate chosen for her. She stood and began pacing the room.

"You're angry. I don't blame you, I would be —"

"Pardon me, but you don't know me well enough to judge my anger. I will bring this man to you, but no one is choosing my mate." She turned on her mother, not sure that this was a smart move on her part, but she was pissed. "Was Ember's mate chosen for her as well? I'm sure that she'll be thrilled to know that her life has been arranged for her."

"No, her finding her mate was a surprise to us all. But this man, Alex, has been chosen as your mate since before he was born. And you will not use that tone with me, young lady. I am still your mother." Storm took a deep breath and then sat down when her mother asked her to.

"I miss said what he was to you, Storm. No one chose him for you. It was written in the tomes of the future. You will mate with him and bring children into this world that will be needed. When I said chosen, I meant that it has been written."

She stalked out of the room and into the courtyard again. This time, she shifted as she ran, her body forming and shaping as she went. By the time she had gone a hundred yards, she was launching herself into the sky and soaring across the night.

~~Enjoy great happiness~~
~~Maintain a fond hope for all kind~~
~~Uphold the reparation of magical energy requirements~~

Storm shifted to a human as she touched the ground. Her body threw off its form as if it were a heavy coat she no longer needed. She had landed close to the mouth of the cave where the man Alex was waiting.

Storm had contacted Ember when she left the Realm late last night. Telling her the events that had happened at the castle, but she left out the part of "the man" being her mate. She did not plan on taking him as her mate, so she felt no reason to relay the news. Storm had also asked Ember to have the man waiting for her at the mouth of the cave. Storm did not want to take the time to go down and get him. The sooner she took him to the Elders and finished this assignment, the happier she would be.

"You're to come with me. I'm to take you to the Chilast," she said when she saw who she assumed was Alexander. She put out her hand to have him come with her.

"I don't think so. Not until someone explains to me what is going on. One minute, I'm on a domestic violence call. The next, I'm being wrapped in wings and brought here. Wings — I've seen some weird shit as a cop, but wings are something I've never encountered before." Alex sat hard onto the stone next to the wall. He looked stubborn and formidable. She was annoyed but impressed, too.

He was a very handsome man and taller than her by a good half a foot. His hair was dark, as dark as Storm's, but where hers was curly, his was straight and hung just past his shoulders. The shirt he had on had been torn, so she had a delicious view of his hard abs and harder chest. It looked smooth, and her fingers itched to touch, not just his chest but his entire body. Storm decided that she did not like him and would not be his mate, no matter what anyone said about it.

"I don't have time to explain, so get ready to go." She could feel the attraction to him, and she hated him all the more for it.

Before he could say anything else, the earth shook beneath them. Alex fell to the cave floor, and Storm was thrown to the wall, striking her head hard. While she fought the blackness trying to consume her, she threw a protective shell around Alex.

"Well, hello, Storm. You have something that belongs to me. I want him. Now!" Grail moved into the mouth opening of the cave, and Storm felt his power surge against the spell she had wrapped around Alex. It wouldn't work, of course, she was much stronger than him, but it would weaken her more in protecting the human.

Grail had been a gray Dragon in color when Storm had first met him, his color bleeding into his human form, giving his eyes and hair the same rich colors. Now, he was black as pitch. His eyes, once a soft, rich, pewter color, were now black with his dark magic and evilness. He was tall, as were all their kind, but he was also heavy. His lack of physical activity not keeping him in the shape he should have been. Though his face, dusky in pallor, was gaunt and shallow. She wondered how he could fly, much less take flight.

"You can't have him. I'm to take him back to the realm." She opened her magic and pushed hard back.

Grail raised his hands, and power appeared in the form of a ball of electricity. The longer he held it, the bigger it grew. If he hit the protection, he would destroy it. Storm needed to get them to safety now.

Storm moved in a flash to stand in front of her assignment; she shifted partway, and her wings fluttered out from her back. She flapped them once, and their powerful movement moved air strongly around the forest and knocked Grail to the ground as he stood in his fragile human form. Turning to Alex, she grabbed him up and ran to the lighted opening just beyond Grail. As she passed him, she felt a searing pain in her back but did not slow her pace. By the time she was in the open light, she was a full dragon, Alex tucked tightly in her talons. She soared high in the air just as Grail screamed at her to come back.

As a dragon, she could see all the areas where it would be safe for them to land. Her vision was perfect, and she could see the heat from any humans or animals below them, not wanting to land where anything could find them. Storm knew she was losing blood, but until she landed and got the man to safety, there was little to nothing she could do. She was getting weaker and knew that she would need to land soon or risk falling and crushing the man she was sent to protect.

Opening her mind, she hoped to be able to speak to the man. It was the way of their kind to be able to talk to their mates when there had been no bond at all between them. Unlike most species, she could have spoken to Alex since his birth had she known about him being what he was to her.

"Are you hurt? I should have asked sooner, but I wanted to get you out of harm's way."

"No. I'm fine. Your claws are digging into me, but I fear that if you lessen your grip, I feel I'll fall to the earth—unless that is your plan? Tell me, Storm, do you plan to play toss the man into the air and see if you can catch him before he plummets to the earth. If so, could we not play today? I have a very busy schedule tomorrow, and if I'm crushed…well, it could put a crimp in things. No, I think a little pinching is preferable to death. I can smell your blood. How hurt are you?" She told him that she was, but she would heal when they landed. "If there is anything I can do to help you, please let me know. I'm pretty handy to have around."

She smiled at his sense of humor. Storm had not expected that. He was being very calm for a man who was being flown well above the clouds by a huge blue dragon.

"I must land soon to sleep and heal. I know of a place where you'll be safe until I can do both. No one will bother you there." She told him with as much reassurance as she could. Weakness was pulling hard at her, and she did not think she could go much longer.

"So you plan to leave me? I hope you don't expect me to sit around quietly waiting for your return. I may not know what is going on or why that other... what was he anyway?"

"He's a dragon like me. And you will stay where I tell you. You are to live at all costs. I don't have time to placate your feelings, human. I can easily say that you were eaten by Grail as not. Now be quiet." Storm began her descent.

Pain racked her body, and she knew that the landing was going to be hard. Seconds before she hit the earth, she dropped Alex and tumbled over him, careful not to land on him. As much as he irritated her, she did not want to kill him.

Her body shifted as soon as she stopped rolling, shifting to the last shape she had taken, hiding her true identity from anyone who would come upon her injured body. It was there to provide their kind with surreptitiousness.

Storm sat up just long enough to ensure that Alex was all right, her body and mind already pulling her to sleep. The area where she had taken them was hers; it was safe and hidden well from everyone, including any of her kind. She saw Alex stand and stride toward her just as blackness pulled her under.

~*~

Alex leaned over the woman he had carried into the house he had found a mile or so from where she had fallen. The fire he had lit in the deep fireplace reflected off her face, the reds and golds of the flames casting surreal shadows across her flawless cheeks. She was a beauty, just like her sister, Ember.

There was no doubt to him that the two women were sisters, as they were identical twins and as alike as any he had ever seen. He moved the dark hair away from her face and ran his fingers down her downy cheek. When she stirred slightly, he grinned. She was by far the most stubborn person he had ever met.

"Why do you look at me like that?" She looked up at him, her voice soft in the hushed room.

"I was thinking about how unlike your sister and you are. You are very beautiful, both of you. But you lack her softness and the...genteel nature that she has. You are strong and stubborn. And I've never wanted to kiss anyone more than I do you."

The expression on her face was priceless. He nearly laughed out loud but caught himself before it burst forth. He was afraid she would hurt him. Alex was not a stupid man, he had seen what she was, and while it was hard to believe, he was not going to dismiss the fact that she had flown them away from trouble.

"Why?" He asked her what she meant. "Why

would you want to kiss me? It's not like I'm all that much. I'm, well, at least for the moment, just a woman who has the ability to change into a great dragon. Nothing special about that."

"Why would I want to kiss you, or why do I think you're stubborn?" He touched her again. He could not seem to help himself. "And you are extremely special. I've only just thought of this too. You're extremely special to me for some reason. Do you know why?"

She looked at him for long moments, and he suddenly felt her touch his mind again, this time in a searching way, not to speak. Alex was not sure why he did not block her, but he would not try to fight her if she needed reassurance.

"You're a vampire. They didn't tell me that." She sat up on the side of the bed, but he didn't move back. It put them closer than before, and he was happy with that.

"Yes, I'm a vampire. You're a dragon. I didn't know that you even existed until I met Ember. You say 'they'. Who? And who is that man who tried to kill us?"

"The Elders of our kind, they are the ones who sent me to bring you back to them. The other dragon, his name is Grail. He's also a dragon like me, a time shifter. Did Ember tell you what we do?" He nodded, and she continued. "He was there to kill you and me because we're supposed to be mates. We are to deliver the next line of dragons. Mother told me that our children were meant to destroy him and his reign. I didn't stick around long enough to hear why. Grail has been building his power base for many years and has been moving through time, making adjustments in the fabric of lives to gather monies to fund his cause — to destroy all dragons but himself. I was in the Americas waiting for Grail to make a move to take a group of scientists away before they were to die, but he came here to get you instead. We had been tracking him for some time. The earthquake that happened in China was the result of him having a temper tantrum. Ember said that she had been sent to save you, but she didn't know why until I spoke to her. You see, you were to die in that last call you went on when on patrol. When Grail realized that you had survived, he unleashed his anger on those people."

"I'm sorry for them. I never meant to cause them harm." He was a good cop, and he never pulled his gun unless it was the only thing left for him to do.

Storm stood up and looked at him. The glow from the fire danced in her eyes. When she licked her lips, he watched, mesmerized by the pink tip moistening her lush lips. "Storm…"

Before he could claim her mouth, he felt himself being tossed across the room. Storm landed across his body, protecting him from falling debris. Her hand clamped tightly across his mouth when he started to speak.

"Grail." She said in a way of explanation. Moving quickly, she stood and pulled him close to her.

"I know you're in there, Storm, my dear. Come out and play with me, and bring our tasty friend along with you. We'll char him up and laugh over the silliness of all this fighting. I can offer you so much more than he could ever."

Alex pressed back against the far wall and flipped Storm around so that her back was now where his had been, and he moved hard to her body.

"As a human, is he as mortal? Will he die like a regular man?" Alex moved the thoughts through her mind. The words were fast and hard, urgent even.

"No. Yes. It needs to be silver through his heart, though. But his dragon would protect him by wrapping himself around Grail and taking him away. Grail would sense your movement, and as quick as you are, Grail is much faster. You can't...you can't think to beat him, do you? He'll take you, kill you."

"Do you care, Storm? Would you morn me if he kills me?" Now, his voice was a caress, a stroke along her heart and mind.

Without hesitation, without speaking in his mind, she answered. "Yes. Yes, I would."

"You are mine, understand?" He warned her. At her nod, he kissed her quickly and pulled his gun from his ankle holster. Winking at her, he took her hand and moved to the front of what had once been a small house.

"Please, Alex, please don't do this. He'll kill you." She whispered in his mind again.

"He'll try." When he started to step away, she pulled him back into the semi-darkness. "What?"

"You need to feed from me. I'll strengthen you, protect you. Feed from me, and my dragon will know you, and it'll keep you safe, keep us both safe."

Alex looked at her and smiled. He felt his fangs drop into place to feed. The need to sip from her nearly staggered him off his feet.

He wanted to savor her, make her his, and knew from her sister that dragon blood, especially Storm's blood, was poison to those who did not ask and were given permission before drinking. But for those who had been allowed that rare sip, the benefits were amazing. Alex leaned into her throat, nuzzling her skin, tasting her with his mouth and tongue. Licking the area just over the pulse pounding in her neck, he pulled back slightly and stuck his bite deep and quick. Her moan ran along his skin like a caress.

At the first taste of her essence, he immediately felt the power surge into him. The more he drew from her, the stronger he felt his body getting. Alex was an older vampire, so his strength was not paltry, but with her surging through his veins, he felt extraordinary.

Pulling back reluctantly, he sealed the tiny wounds with a flick of his tongue. Moving his mouth along her jaw, he reached her mouth and sealed his over her heat.

"I know that you're in there, Storm. I demand that you come out now and face me. I have plans for us, plans that do not include that vampire mate of yours. Children of our union will bring me more money than I ever imagined."

Alex backed away from her slightly and saw the lust in her eyes. "If you stay right here, I'll take care of him, and we can get back to where we were before he interrupted us."

"I need to keep you safe. I need to stand at your side." He smiled at her possessive tone.

Moving and taking her hand once again, he hid his gun behind him as they walked forward.

"Ah, the future Queen and her stud. You know, I think I'm going to enjoy killing him. Oh yeah, this is going to be..."

He never finished. As he dropped to the ground, Grail stared at the smoking gun in Alex's hand.

Alex and Storm watched as Grail began to shift into several forms quickly before he just simply melted into the ground; his blue blood stained the ground beneath him.

There was a lot to be said for the element of surprise.

Chapter 1

Tabby watched as the workers for the new warehouse put the finishing touches on the building. While that was going on, there were big bulldozers flattening out the last of the parking lot, too. It was coming along so nicely that she felt her excitement for it nearly overwhelm her again. Hugging her daughter, she was excited as she was.

"Hello, my darling Mandy. How's my favorite granddaughter doing this fine day?" She told him that she was his only granddaughter, and they hugged. "So how does this work, Tabby? I know you said that we don't own the land around here but are getting a tax abatement as well as free rent for the first five years. I don't understand how they're going to be making any kind of money when all this work is going into this place." She looked at her dad and couldn't help but smile at him. He was as excited as she was. "Your mother is terrified that we're not going to be able to afford the rent once this place is finished and the terms are finished up."

"They own the land to be built on. I've mentioned

that. But once we get up and running, they'll ease their way of getting money from us every six months. We'll start out by paying ten grand a month for six months, then it will go to twenty grand. This also has us paying the taxes on the land after five years, too. We're going to be making out well for this, Dad." He asked her if she'd had an attorney go over the contracts. "I have. And the only loophole that he could find was in our favor. He even told me that we'd be foolish if we didn't sign off on this deal they're giving us. Dad, we're going to be able to triple our business in less than a year with this warehouse here."

"You know how your mother worries." She knew how he worried, too. After assuring him that things were going well, he just nodded at her and told her that she'd done a good job with the expansion. "How many people are we going to be able to hire over the next five years, and do you think that it'll be easy to get them to work for us?"

"I have over five thousand applicants now. I've already hired about two hundred to start the first day we can get into the building and start setting up the lines to the bay doors. Then, the shelving units. Did I tell you that more than half the building is refrigerated? That's going to help us keep things fresher for a lot longer. Not to mention the amount of room we're going to have. I'm excited about the drivers we have, too. The highway is only four miles away with exit and on ramps just down the road from here." Dad asked her if she had someone to run it. "That's going to be up to you and mom. It's your decision whether or not one of us, myself and my brothers, run the place here, leaving you and Mom, and I was thinking one of us there to help you in Tennessee."

"You want it here, don't you?" She told him that she did. More than anything. "I thought as much. I know you're here every day looking the plans over. Your mom said that you've been going over the blueprints daily to make sure that nothing is being left out."

"I love it here. And so does Mandy. And housing isn't all that expensive, not like it is at home." She looked at the construction going on. "It's something that I've been working on since the beginning. I'm the one that got the contracts and started this up. But I want you to know that there won't be any trouble from me if you decide to go with Earl or Tommy. I know they're older than me."

"They might be older than you are, sweetheart, but they don't have the heart you have when it comes to this company. I think that even they can see it. Earl has even told me that I'd be a fool if I didn't have you running the plant here." She asked what Tommy had to say about it. "He wants out. I knew he was headed in that direction for a few years now. I think that he messes up just so I'll fire him. I can't do that."

"I could fire him. Easily. And because I know he wants out too, I'd be able to make it, so there're no hard feelings." Dad just nodded and continued to look over the construction site. "Dad, what is it? You're not excited about this expansion?"

"I'm very excited for the expansion. It's what I've dreamed of for a good long time. Not only that, but I'm excited to see how quickly we outgrow this building. I'm betting that in five years or less, you'll be talking to someone about getting more space than you'll have now."

"You're sounding like I've got this place." He winked at her. "I don't know what that means. You're going to have to sound out your words for me, Dad."

"You've had this place since before we came home from vacation. I think you'd be very hurt too if I didn't make sure that you were here too, even though you said you'd not." She hugged her dad and then hugged him a second time. "The people that you're working with on this end of the deal seem to have it in their heads that it was a done deal even before the first shovel of dirt was dug up. That was kinda fun. Having the press there when we broke ground."

"I'm glad they were willing to wait for you and Mom to come home before they did that. Earl would have done it, but he didn't want to be in the limelight. He's never enjoyed being the center of attention, has he?" Dad pointed out that she didn't care for it either. "No, but I can do it if it comes to having a place where jobs are going to be happening, and we get to triple our business."

"I love you, Tabby girl. You've done us up proud with this. I hope you know too how proud your mother and I are." She said she got it. "Good. Why don't you come home with me, Mandy girl, and we have some lunch, just the two of us."

When Mandy agreed with her grandpa, she knew that his day had been made better. He dearly loved her daughter, and Mandy loved her grandpa. Their lives were going to be better from now on, too.

They watched the construction working for another half hour before they got in her car and made their way back to the hotel they'd been staying at. They talked about her getting a home large enough to accommodate them all when they came for a visit, too. She was just telling her dad about how it was only an eight-hour drive to the new plant from where she grew up when her cell phone rang. It was Amy, who she'd been working with all along.

"I heard your parents were in town. I was wondering if we could all meet for dinner tonight and have a celebration. According to the man in charge at the warehouse, they'll have the building finished just as soon as the inspection goes through, all right?" She put the phone on speaker after asking if it was all right so that Amy could repeat what she'd said. "Dinner would be great since we've yet to talk to you in person, Mr. Reader."

"Please call me Sheppard. Yes, it would be nice to be able to put a face to the voice I've been talking to for months now. I met your husband just a few days ago when we were talking about the employee breakrooms. Dinner sounds good, so long as you allow us to pay. You've put yourself out there enough already." Amy said it would be their treat as she was the one who asked for it. "We'll talk about that when we get together. My wife and two sons are in the area, too, to give you a heads up."

"That's fine. I have five brothers-in-law, with those that are married to their wives, too. We're a big happy family." Dad mouthed a question to her about how many were married. She told him three. Not that she'd met the single ones yet, but she knew about them. After giving them the address where the restaurant was, Amy said that she'd see them tonight and rang off. Dad looked at her.

"You said they weren't human. Do you know what they are?" She said that she didn't, but did it really matter? "No, not at all. But whatever they are, they're good people, and that's all I care about. Tell me something, honey, have they approached you about being mates to any of them?"

"No. Goodness, Dad, are you trying to get me married off? No thanks. I have enough on my plate right now." They both laughed. Dad had an unusual sense of humor, she thought. "Seriously, if one of them is my mate, I'm going to give up this place and move back home. I do not need to have some man telling me how to live my life."

"And I think we had enough of that with that Levi person that locked us in the house and had us doing everything he wanted." She looked at Mandy in the mirror. "No thanks, please. Once was quite enough for me."

"All right, honey. I was only joking, anyway. But it would do me a world of good to have you settled like Earl is. You know that he's just as much a homebody as I am. It'll be nice to get him out more, don't you think?" She asked him about Tommy. "Tommy will be lucky if a woman will date him twice for the way he treats women. I have no idea where he got his ideas about women from, but someone is going to hand him his ass soon if he doesn't settle down and take care to keep his mouth shut."

She'd noticed that about Tommy as well. He had this idea that women should be naked, barefooted, and in the kitchen. He didn't want any kids, but he wanted a subservient woman to take care of him, and that just wasn't going to happen. At least, she hoped not. Her brother was hard enough to live with as it was now.

Going back to the hotel, they made arrangements to have a limo come and pick them up before dinner. The woman at the desk said that she knew the restaurant they were going to and they had good food. She also told them that they were usually up for private rooms as well. Tabby didn't know if they'd have something like that as Amy was taking care of the arrangements for the place, but it would be nice to have a room all to themselves while there. They needed to get together and meet, and that would make it perfect.

Going to her room, she decided that it was early enough that she could get a nice nap in. Mandy said she was going to take one as well and laid down on the other bed. Neither of them had been sleeping all that well, and it was starting to pull her down. After setting her phone alarm and having the hotel call her so she could get up in time, Tabby stripped down to her panties and bra and laid out on the bed. It was no time at all when she felt herself drifting off to sleep.

Waking up when the phone rang for the alarm, she was a little worried when she didn't know where she was. Once she got it settled in her mind, she got up to take a nice shower. Mandy was already dressed and ready. While she didn't know what her parents were going to be wearing, she decided to wear a nice warm skirt and sweater so she'd not be chilly. The temperature had been dropping once the sun went down, and she didn't want to be too cold on the way home. The limo pulled up in front of the hotel just as she was getting off the elevator with her family.

"How much do you know about this family, Tab?" She told Earl that the only people she'd been talking to were Amy and her husband, Fowler. The others she didn't know all that well at all. "I've been reading up on them. They're supposed to be like the richest people in the world. Billionaires several times over, I read."

"Amy told me once that they were doing all right financially. That's why they were giving us such a good deal on the plant we're building." She told them all some of the other perks that, as a business, they'd be getting. Some that she'd not even told her dad about. "I never bothered with looking them up—I suppose that I should have before signing any of the contracts, but I have a gut feeling about them that makes me think they're going to be the perfect partners to go into business with. I believe that our attorneys would have looked into their background before okaying the contracts. That's what we pay them for, correct?"

They pulled up in front of the restaurant just as

the others were going inside. Good, she thought, they didn't have to wait around for them to be there. And they did have a private room, which from the looks of all the place settings on the table was going to be quite the crowd of them having dinner."

~*~

Edgar was running behind. He hated to be late for things, and this dinner was important to the family. But there were things that just kept him from leaving work early enough to go home and change. He reached out to his brother to ask if he should come on in or just wait until the next time they were in town to have dinner.

"How far are you out?" He told Fowler that he was about twenty minutes from the place. And in that time, he'd have to run home and change out of his jeans and shirt. "Come like you are. If anyone gives you any shit, like Mom or Dad, I'll take the heat for it. I explained how important this was for all of us, didn't I?"

"You did, but I got hung up at the hospital on one of the things you had me checking out. I swear to you, Fowler, there is some hinky shit going on there that I can't wait to talk to you about." He told him that they'd talk later but to hurry. "I'm pulling into the lot right now, so I should only be about another three minutes tops."

He was able to time it well by having a seat at

the table with his part of the family. They were nice-looking people, and as soon as he sat down, he looked at his parents and winked. They didn't look upset with him, but perhaps he might still be in trouble. Fowler introduced him to the others at the table, telling them that he'd been working up until a few minutes ago.

"I didn't know you gentlemen had jobs." Sheppard, as he was introduced to him by that name, said he was sorry. "I shouldn't have said that. We were just talking about how much you're worth on the way in here. Please don't take offense."

"I didn't. And yes, we're wealthy beyond anyone's dreams, but we still work daily. I have a job of keeping the charities straight and how they're using the money that we donate. Reading over contracts to that might cross our desks at some point. We don't toss our money at anything without keeping an eye on it." He asked if they'd have that much time invested in the warehouse. "Of course. It wouldn't be mine to watch over, but Amy and Fowlers. But that doesn't mean that we all won't have a vested interest in it. I might be asked to go over the books at some point—if there is a problem. I'm not saying that there will be; I'm just saying that we all keep track of what we invest in. It's a family project like everything else we do."

"I like that idea. I might not have lost so much money when I first started investing had I taken as

much care as your family does about investments. I
didn't lose my shirt, but enough that it stung a little
when they went belly up after two years." Edgar
waited to speak until after his and Sheppard's orders
were taken. He asked him if he had anyone investing
in his family. "I consider the warehouse an investment.
Even though it's ours, I can see the potential of doing
it right the first time. However, I will tell you this, I'm
nervous about this project of my daughters. It's a great
deal of money."

"On that project, I'm a little more aware of
things. I was asked to do the projected sales of the
place over the next five years, then ten more down
the road. You're doing the right thing. It will increase
your leverage of hitting all the markets with a thirty
percent increase in sales you have now. And over the
next ten years, you're looking at about another sixty
percent increase on top of the thirty you've already.
The money that you've put into this deal will be back
into your accounts by year seven. That's one hell of an
investment, and whoever started it should get a raise."

"Thank you. You've no idea how much hearing
that from someone else means to me. I'm not as young
as I used to be, and making up for the losses of this
investment would hurt badly at this point in my life."
He told him he was going to be in good hands. "So my
daughter keeps telling me. She tells me all the time that

she knows what she's doing with this, and I want to believe her, but like I said, I'm not as young as I used to be."

"You're going to be just fine. She'll do right by you because she can think outside the box." He told him how his older son doesn't think outside the lines at all. "Then he'll fail."

Sheppard laughed. "Are you always so honest about your speaking?" He told him that regarding money, he was forever serious. "Yes, I suppose you would need to be as wealthy as I've read that you are. We know that you're not human, but exactly what are you?"

"Dragon." He took his salad from the waitstaff and looked over at Sheppard when he seemed to be frozen in staring at him. Taking the salad, he nudged the man a little to get him going and then handed off the part of his meal that was in his hand. "Do you have a problem with us being dragons, sir?"

"Problem? No. I don't...you're dragons, all of you?" Edgar nodded and said that with the exception of the wives of his brothers, everyone at the table in his family were dragons. "I've never...what I mean is I never...a dragon? Are you larger than...please forgive me. I'm trying to imagine you changing into a great dragon. You're large, aren't you?"

"We are." He let the man stare at him for a

few seconds before he turned and looked at him. "I can show you mine if you'd like. I mean, we'd have to go outside. I think that the people that own this place would be a little pissy if I shifted in their place of business."

Sheppard let go of a small burst of laughter. Then, the longer he sat there, the more he laughed. Edgar wasn't sure if he was thinking he was joking or not, but it was funny to see the man lose control of his mirth. Finally, he slapped him on the back and told him that he liked him. Edgar told him that he liked him as well. Tucking into his salad, he was going to make sure that he was able to show the elderly man his dragon if he didn't do anything else.

The rest of the family was scattered throughout the dining area. He noticed that the daughter, he thought her name was Tabby, was sitting by the women in the family. Mom and Dad hadn't been able to make the dinner, but he was sure that his mom would be having as much fun as the women all seemed to be. Earl, the oldest son of Sheppard and his wife Gina, seemed to be taking cues from his sister and enjoying talking to his brothers.

Tommy, the middle child, was a flirt. He didn't much care for the way that he was treating the staff, treating them like they were only there to serve him, but since he wasn't going to have much to do with this project, he kept his mouth shut. However, if he touched one of the staff again like she'd asked him not to, he was going to say something to his father. Men like Tommy gave the term wealthy a bad name.

Just as the dinners were coming into the room, he'd had enough. Turning to his father, he told Sheppard that the young man was getting too personal with the staff. Something occurred to him as Sheppard stood up to talk to his son, and he had a look on his face that told him this wasn't a one-time offense. Then Tommy whelped like he was in pain.

"Behave." Tabby hissed the word to her brother and had a hold on his ear that might have been comical if not for the fact that she was making him listen to her. "Behave yourself, Thomas Reader, or you can go home right now. These people are our guests. You know for a fact that I won't put up with your shenanigans. Leave the staff alone or go home. That's your only two opinions."

"I was just having a bit of fun with them." She twisted his ear, and that had him complaining again. "All right. I'll behave myself. Christ, when is it against the law to have some fun?"

"It's against the law when you harass someone who is working for you, and since she's bringing you your dinner, she's officially working for you." Tabby sat back down and turned to look at her mother. "He's going to be lucky some waitstaff isn't going to be spitting in his dinner at the rate he's going."

He might well have handled it differently, but he was glad that it was taken care of. Tommy had been patting their asses and making lude comments since he'd sat down. When his father looked in his direction, Tommy shrugged, and Sheppard whispered for him to behave himself, too. It seemed that the entire family knew what they were dealing with in the younger son.

After empty plates were taken away, that opened the discussion to the warehouse. They usually never spoke about business at the table, and today, other than him telling Sheppard he was in good hands, it wasn't discussed. But almost as soon as the last dirty plate was taken away, Tabby stood up and handed out file folders to everyone at the table.

"I wanted everyone to know where the progress is on the warehouse." She handed her dad one, and then him and their fingers brushed. That was all it took for him to know what she was to him. And Christ, oh mighty, she was his mate.

The rest of the conversation was a blur for him. All his mind could center on was that she was right here in the room with him, and he couldn't talk to her. As she went on about how the warehouse was coming along nicely, a week ahead of the planned finish date, he realized that he didn't have a house nor even a stick of furniture to put in one. Just as he was started to hyperventilate, he looked at his brother when he said his name.

"Are you all right? You've gone pale, and your breathing is labored." He nodded, then shook his head. "What the hell is wrong with you? You're looking like you've lost your marbles."

He looked at the table and then back at Melbourne. "She's my mate. I think she's my mate anyway." Melbourne asked him how did he know. "I don't know. That's why I said I think she is. But I have this overwhelming need to protect her from her family. Not to mention, I need to touch her. Is that her being my mate?"

"I don't know. I don't have one, you nutball. But you look like you're freaking out. Stop it." He thought that was a good idea but couldn't think beyond wanting to touch her. "Fowler is going to kill you if you embarrass him like you're doing. Just breathe before I have to slap the piss out of you to make you not pass out. In and out, you idiot."

He thought that he was breathing all right until Melbourne pinched his thigh under the table. The sharp intake of breath made him realize that not only was he not breathing right, but he seemed to be gasping for air; he was deprived of breath. Coughing to cover up what was really going on, Fowler asked him what the hell he was doing.

"I don't know. I think Tabby is my mate. When she touched me just now, I had this overwhelming need to touch her more. Not to mention protecting her from her dumbass brother. Don't be pissy with me. I'm doing the best that I can right now. I feel like I'm messing up, and I don't have any idea why. Is that right?"

Fowler didn't say anything for several minutes, and he had a feeling that he was talking to Amy. Or their parents. Whatever he was doing, it wasn't helping him from being freaked the fuck out. When he finally did speak, it was as if he'd taken some kind of chill pill and was talking to him in a nice, calming voice.

"She's your mate. Congratulations. Just keep breathing in and out, and you'll be fine. We can talk after this meeting. All right?" He thanked him. "You're going to be all right, Edgar. Just try and remain calm so you don't freak out your mate. She's already eyeing you like you have four heads." He looked at her just in time to see her glaring at him. "Just smile...no, don't smile. You don't do fake smiles well, and she might well think you're leering at her. Just, I don't know, just sit there and behave for a half hour or so, and you'll be able to talk to her. Calmly, Edgar. Don't freak out on her, or you'll be worse off than I was when I first found Amy."

"I don't want that at all. You really were a major fuck up." Fowler thanked him, and it sounded so sarcastic that it did make him feel better. "All right, I'm better now. Thanks."

When Fowler found out that Amy was his mate, he ordered her around like she was a simpleton. Then, when she couldn't take it anymore, she got her revenge in a sweet way. It was a wonder to all of them that they'd ever been able to make it work between them the way that Fowler had been acting. Now they were not only good paired mates, but he thought that they were best friends as well. And that was the kind of relationship he wanted with his mate. To be friends as well as lovers.

By the time the meeting ended, he was all right with the way things were going. He must have reassured Tabby as well because she was no longer glaring at him but smiling when he asked a question. He'd had plenty to ask her, too, since he'd gone over the paperwork. He knew about as much as she did about the plant and its profit margins over the next few years. He was actually excited about the venture now that he knew he could if she would allow it to work side by side with her if she needed him.

Waiting to talk to her after Amy did, he looked around the room at the state of affairs it was in. It needed to have an overhaul. There were also cobwebs in the corners and some dust over the light fixtures. It wasn't gross by any means. He had a bit of dust in his apartment, too. But the carpet needed to be replaced, and a few of the tables were wobbly. Yes, the room needed a makeover. He'd talk to the —

"Did you want to talk to me?" Tabby speaking to him pulled him away from what he'd been thinking about the room. "I'm wanting to go home and go to bed if it's all right with you."

"I'm sorry you're here so late. I did want to talk to you, but it can wait until you're rested." She told him to tell her what was going on earlier. "I came to a realization. What do you know about shifters in general?"

"A bit. We have a lot of them that work for us." He nodded. He could smell them on her. Bear, tiger, and a wolf. "What's your point?"

"I belong to you. I mean, we're mates." Nodding when she shook her head, he told her that they were. "I'm not as positive as I might have been earlier, but now that I'm standing next to you, I'm sure. Your scent calls to my other half."

"Not that I believe you, but what sort of shifter are you? And if you tell me that you can't discuss this with me, I'm going to smack you around like I did with my brother." He asked her why he'd not be able to discuss it with her. "We have this one shifter that works for us, and he claims that he isn't supposed to tell people what he is. I know what others we have working for us, but he's so secretive about it that it makes me want to fire him."

"Have you been around him much in the last few days?" She said that just before coming in here, she had gotten the files from him. "May I smell your hands? I can tell what he is without him knowing."

Not only did he smell her hands but the file that she had in her hands, too. It took him two tries until he finally was able to tell her that he was nothing more than a human.

"Why would he tell me he's a shifter then?" He said he didn't know but asked her a couple of questions so that he might be able to tell her why he was doing that. "No, he doesn't ask for special time off, but I've never seen him lift anything more heavy than a ream of paper. And he complains about that."

"I have no idea what sort of worker he is, but I'd get rid of him for the simple reason that he's lied to you. If you can't trust him, then that is as good a reason as any to get him out before he does something to harm your business or you. I'm a dragon, by the way." She nodded, then looked at him with a cocked brow. "You don't believe me? I don't think your dad did either. He thought it was too funny for me to be one."

"I have no reason not to believe you, but I know

nothing at all about your kind." He told her that few people did. "I guess I can understand that as well. The less people know — don't tell my brother Tommy. Here, of late, I don't trust him with a lot of things going on around me. Also, I don't really care how you feel about this, but I have a daughter. She's my number one priority over anything else."

"As she should be, and I will protect her like I will you. But about your brother, that's not good. If you don't mind me asking, what has he done to lose your trust?" She pointed out tonight for one thing and that he keeps doing things to upset the normal way of things going on at the first warehouse. "You mean the buying of the days-old fruit and the salmon?"

"One of many, yes." He told her that he'd look into a couple of things and get back with her. "All right. But what about us? I mean, I'm not even sure there is an us, but I'm too busy to try and figure out what you want from me."

"Nothing at all that you're not sure you want to give me." She looked skeptical. "Why don't we talk more tomorrow. You're exhausted, and I need to get some things finished up, too. I'll be in the hotel lobby tomorrow, and the three of us can have breakfast together. All right?"

She agreed, and he followed her out. But he kept an eye on her brother. There was something off about him, and he'd figure it out for her. Tomorrow. He needed to get home, too.

Chapter 2

Earl watched his brother while he was in the warehouse. He'd come home only this morning with him, and he was talking about how he wanted the business to be run better. He couldn't get out of him how it was going to be run better, just that he did. As far as Earl was concerned, Tommy had been let go of the company so that he could pursue his own dreams. Whatever that might be.

"Did Tabby tell you how much we made off the day-old stuff I got for nearly nothing? Then there was the fish. I didn't know it was salmon, but she was able to sell it all off to one person. They knew they were getting a good deal too and bought it all up." Earl asked him what that had to do with running the business better. "We could make a lot of profit off of buying and selling some of the fruits and vegetables that are sitting on the dock for too long."

"Yes, but we make a good profit off of selling fresh too. I don't want to be known as the man who sells old stuff when we have a business of selling good fruits. It's called Reader's Fresh for a reason." Tommy said he wasn't seeing the whole picture. "I don't think you're seeing anything but profit, and the little bit of profit that Tabby made off of the stuff you got was because one person bought it all. Had we had to be selling it out by a person that just happened to come by, we might well have been in the hole."

"I sent out flyers on the websites to all the people that we work with." He told his brother that Tabby had had to put up with calls all day with people wanting her to sort through it all and take out the good stuff. It interfered with her work. "She wouldn't do it. She told people, our customers, that she wasn't going to go sort through the pallets to see what was out there. That's pretty shitty of her if you were to ask me."

"Why didn't you stick around and do it for her? You're the one who bought the stuff. You should have been the one to deal with it if you were to ask me." He pointed out that she was here. "So were you, Tommy. Why did you even do it in the first place? You know that we don't sell old stuff. That was pretty shitty, as you said of you to drop that onto her plate when she was getting orders sorted that people pay us to do."

He waved him off. "Well, as of two days ago, I'm in charge of this warehouse, and Tabby is in charge of the one in Ohio. Don't do that again. I won't allow you to go out after you bought it. If you buy shit like that, you're going to be dealing with it. And there will be no charging things to the company again either. We still haven't been able to get an invoice from the company you purchased that stuff from."

"Dad said that I was off the hook for being responsible for the things that come and go here and there. But I'm still a working family member, Earl. Don't forget it." He asked him if he was threatening him. "I don't think that's the way I meant it, but if you're going to treat me badly, I'm going to start working badly around here."

"Go home, Tommy." He just sat there. "I mean it. Go home and talk to Dad about what you've been doing here. I bet he'll say the same thing. Not to do it anymore so that we're not left holding the bag—or, in this case, a lot of things that we can't get rid of before it all goes bad."

When he finally left after sweeping paperwork to the floor, Earl cleaned up his mess and finished with the orders that were to go out tomorrow. They had to be at least a day ahead on the things going out and coming in, or they'd never get any work done. Just as he was closing the office for the day, hardly realizing that it was well after seven, he got a call from his dad.

"Not that I believe him, but Tommy told me that you ran him off when he was working today. Good for you." He said that he had run him off, but he wasn't working. "I didn't think so. You'd not do that to him.

He also said that he was going to go up and work with his sister. Tabby won't put up with him either. He's saying some very strange things about how Tabby works."

"He told me too that he's not happy with the way Tabby handled the day-old stuff that he got for the warehouse. He seems to think she did him dirty by not going out and separating out the stuff for customers when they asked. I can imagine what she said to him, too. It was his mess, and she wasn't going to go the extra mile in doing work for him. What's with him lately?" Dad said he didn't know, but he was starting to notice that he wasn't working out very well. "Speaking of not working out very well, I've fired Shamus West. He's been telling us that he's a shifter since he's been working here. He's been lying about a lot of things about himself. And I got rid of him this morning when I came in. He was pitching a fit about how he was forever the only one that worked around here. I didn't fire him for not being a shifter but for lying all the time. I didn't want him in the office if I can't trust him."

"Good. I know that Tabby was thinking of doing the same thing to him. Good thing that Edgar told her that he was only a human. Can't trust people to work in the office if you can't trust them to be truthful about what they are." Dad must have gone someplace quieter because it suddenly got quiet where he was. "I have a couple of things that I need to talk to you about. Now, I'm not blaming anyone about this, but there are over ten grand missing from the ledgers from last month. Have you seen Tommy with a lot of cash?"

"You think he'd rob us?" Earl had to sit down. To think that his own family would rob them was just crazy. "Dad, that's a lot of money to be missing, yes, but do you really think that Tommy would take it?"

"He's not worked any for the last eight weeks, so there was no check for him from the business. Then, last night, I heard that he was all caught up on his rent now. I'm not saying that he took it, but it seems suspicious that it's missing, and he's suddenly flush with cash." Earl asked him if he'd talked to him about it. "I only found out this morning when I got back to the office. I'm worried, Earl. Very much so. And if he took this, it's going to look bad on him when we have to have an audit."

"I'll talk to him. Usually, I can talk to him better when it's just the two of us. Tabby can, too, but I think she'd just come right out and tell him that he'd taken the money to see if he'd deny it or not." Dad laughed, telling him that she didn't suffer fools easily. "She barely suffers anyone easily. For someone that works in the public, she sure is a ball buster when she needs to be."

"That she is. Reminds me of my dad all the time. He would have made Tommy confess like she would. Anyway, I wanted to talk to you about your sister too. I just found out that she's the mate of one of the Walsh men. Edgar Walsh." He asked if he was upset by that. "No. I'm sort of thrilled, to be honest. She deserves happiness, and I know they're a good family. But he told me that he's a dragon. I don't know if I believe him or not."

"They are. I heard about them while I was up there for the dinner. Most of the townspeople know that, but they don't care because of the help they get from them. I guess they donate a lot of money to the schools and other charity banks. The food that they purchased from us went to homes that could use the extra for growing families. They even work with their local pack to help with jobs for them, too." Dad asked him if anyone had seen their dragons. "I doubt they just shift into one of them without a lot of fanfare. I don't know how big they are, but in my head, I have it that they're huge. I wouldn't want to mess with any of those men, shifter or not."

"Yes, they do look like they bench press cars for fun." Earl laughed with his dad. "I'd like to see one of them. Just because you know they aren't around where you can see them. I mean, there used to be a story going around that the skies were black with them flying around. I'd just like to see one up close and personal." Dad laughed again.

They talked for a bit more until Dad told him to come home for dinner. After telling him that he had plans tonight, he told him that he wanted to hear from him about what happened with Tommy. He assured him that he'd get with him afterward for sure. But he thought maybe they should run it by Tabby, too, so she has a heads-up. They both agreed that she needed to know as well.

Earl had a date tonight. He wasn't looking forward to it and couldn't for the life of him remember why he'd agreed to go out in the first place. Donna was someone that he'd met at the bank a couple of weeks ago, and the next several times he'd come into the bank, she was the teller that he'd dealt with. So, on a whim, he supposed he had asked her out. Tonight had been agreed on by both parties.

He was getting his tie straightened out when Tabby called him. "I won't keep you long, but I have two questions. What do you know about the Walsh family, and how much do you know about dragon shifters?" Earl answered both questions with a short I don't know to both. "Yeah, I have a rundown on their background from the check we did on them, but nothing personal. I like them all, but Edgar says that he's my mate, that he belongs to me, or something along those lines."

"That's the way it should be. That he belongs to you." She asked him why. "Did he say that he owns you? No, he didn't. That sounds to me like he's telling you that he's not going to be ruling you around or anything like that. You also don't have to worry about him, just being out for your money. He has a great deal more than we'll ever have. Why? Did something happen?"

"I'm having dinner with him tonight if I can find my clothes so that we can talk and get to know one another. Mandy is staying with Mom and Dad tonight. I'm all for it, but I got to thinking. I don't even know what sort of questions to ask him about being a wealthy man/dragon. Would you?" He was in his car when he told her that he'd just let things flow. "Yeah, I figured that if he didn't tell me something that I want to know, I can just keep at him until he does. Dad doesn't believe he's a dragon."

"He told me." Starting his car, he sat there thinking for a minute. "Dad wants to see his dragon. I'm assuming that at some point, you'll see him, too. Just tell Dad what you've seen, and he'll be thrilled. But I have a date."

"Good for you. I'm happy for you. All right, I'll get off here with you. Tomorrow, we'll compare notes on how our dates go. But you sound less than thrilled about yours, and I'm excited and nervous about mine. I love you, Earl." He told her that he loved her as well. "Really, you have fun tonight, and I'll try very hard not to piss off my dragon."

He was still laughing when he finally put the car into drive and headed to Donna's home. He'd bet anything that Tabby's date would be more fun, so he decided to have as much fun as he could as well. He didn't want his little sister to have more fun than him on a stupid date.

As soon as she opened her door, he knew that it wasn't going to work out. He wasn't looking for long-term, but he was looking for someone to be able to have a nice dinner with or go to the movies with. Donna was dressed in a dress that was fit for high society, and he was in jeans, a shirt, and tie.

"I thought that you'd be more dressed up." He asked her why they were just having dinner. "You said that we were going to dinner, and I thought that we'd try one of the nicer restaurants in town. Someplace that we can be seen."

"I don't understand." But he did. She wanted to be seen with him as a potential mate or whatever she was calling them. "I'm pretty sure that people will see us at Hudson's. You might be slightly overdressed, but we can still have fun. I think that Friday nights are line dancing night."

"I don't know how to line dance. Do you?" He didn't but nodded at her anyway. It didn't seem that hard, and he figured he'd give it a shot just to have a bit of fun with her. "Well, I don't want to go there. As I said, I wanted to go someplace special. Like with a wine list and cloth napkins. Hudson's is mostly a bar, isn't it?"

"They have one, yes. But I think their menu is pretty extensive, too. I've been there a few times." And while he did enjoy himself. He'd only been with his sister and brother, and Tabby could make anything fun. "If you don't want to go out, that's all right too. I think that we had a miscommunication about this date all the way around, don't you?"

"You had a miscommunication. I knew what I wanted when you asked me out." She still hadn't come out of her house, and he was getting bored with standing on her porch. "I want to go someplace nicer than Hudson's. If you want to go home and change, we can start over."

"I don't have reservations anywhere." She huffed at him. "I don't know why you thought that we'd be going someplace nicer than Hudson's when this is our first date."

"Because you have money." And there it was. The tell all of dates, he has money, and she wanted a bit of it. Even if it was on a date. "I'm not going to

Hudson's with you. In fact, I think this whole dating thing isn't going to work out for either of us. Unless you go home and change into something better, I'm going to go inside and be pissy with you until you make things right for us."

"Okay, first of all, there is no us. I asked you out because I thought you'd be fun. Secondly, just because I asked you out doesn't mean that I'm going to be spending hundreds of dollars on you on a first date. This is for us to get to know one another to see if there is another date."

"Well. I never." He was actually happy that she was showing her true colors now instead of during dinner. "I'm going to let it be known to all my friends that you're a cheapskate when it comes to having a date with. To think that I got all dressed up for you only to be disappointed. Well, go home. I'm going to make it so you never find another date so long as you're alive." He couldn't help himself. He asked her if that meant that he wasn't going to get a good night kiss. She slammed the door in his face for an answer.

~*~

Tabby met him at the door when he rang her doorbell. "I've only just moved into my house, and I can't find any of my dress-up clothing. So I thought that we'd just eat here. I made pasta. Is that all right?" He grinned at her, and she smiled back. "I guess I could have been nicer in the way I answered the door. But I really have been living out of boxes for the last two days, and it's not going as well as one might think."

"It's fine. I think it would be a lot less chaotic if we just ate here. And I love pasta." She allowed him to come in and took his jacket. "It's supposed to rain later tonight, so I brought a jacket to wear." He shook his head. "I'm nervous, too, if you can't tell."

"I've been on pins and needles all day. Thank you for putting me at ease." She asked him to sit in the living room. "The plant is coming along nicely. I was there most of the day. I would have come home earlier, but I got caught up in the shelves going up and forgot the time."

"I've been working on several projects for my parents. They're the ones that are working with Amy and my brother in the food distribution. They were inspected this morning, and they got an 'a' reading, so that's all good. How was your day otherwise getting caught up in the day?" She told him how she'd been in touch with her family now that they'd all gone home. "I bet you already miss them. I know I would my family if we were that far apart."

"I do miss having them around so that I can talk to them when I want. I bet that you guys are forever in touch with each other with that shifter thing." He told her that they use it a great deal. "Is there any kind of limit on how far away you can be when you talk to them?"

"No. My mom is the queen of the land and in another realm. I can talk to her, and I do talk to her anytime that I want. We're a very close family." She asked him about his mom being the queen of the other land. Her fear hiked up a bit. She didn't need a madman in her life again. She was still getting over what Levi did to her. "I want you to meet them all. I know that you think I'm a little off, but I assure you that I am a dragon and that my mother is the queen of faeries and other creatures. In fact, I have one of them for you. Here. This is Punch. He's been able to pick his name because he's going to hang out with you to keep you safe."

There was nothing in his hand, and she was getting more nervous by the second. She liked him and didn't want him to be off his meds. Standing up when the timer went off, she was moving toward the kitchen when she saw a flash of something go by her. Before she could get her bearings, something flashed by her once again.

"He's working to get you to see him. His name is Punch, and if you'd have a seat, I'll check on dinner for you." When he stood up, he took her hand into his and put it out like something was going to be put into it. Watching her hand, fearful of him hurting her, she looked up at Edgar when he said her name. "He's yellow and blue. He'll protect you from any harm that comes your way by just being with you. Look at him. He's right there in the palm of your hand, Tabby. I promise you, I'm not crazy."

"I don't know what to do." She looked at her hand and saw something that was blue and sparkling. "Edgar, there is glitter in my hand. Did you do that?"

"I didn't. You're beginning to see him now. He's very sparkly. Punch has blue and yellow wings, too, that are fluttering quickly on his back. He's about four inches tall and very nice. I promise you, he's as real as I am. As real as you are, too."

She saw him then, a little man was standing on her hand and smiling at her. When her knees got weaker, she felt rather than saw Edgar move to help her be seated. He was telling her that he had her while this little person stood on her hand and watched her.

"I can see him," she whispered to Edgar. "He's right here in my hand. And he's very blue and yellow. Like neon blue and yellow."

"Hello, my lady. My name is Punch. I named myself that because when I was smaller and a house faerie, there was a show on called Punch and Judy that my mistress loved to watch." She nodded, still holding onto Edgar. "I shall never harm you, my lady. I'm, as Lord Edgar said, here to protect you. I can be very helpful when you learn what magic that you have, too."

"I'll have magic?" She looked at Edgar again when the little person only nodded his head. "I don't know that I'd need magic, do you?"

"You'll have all kinds of it now and more later. Right now, you should be able to change your clothing at will. Just think of something that you'd rather be wearing, and it'll appear on you." She thought of sweatpants and a sloppy sweatshirt, and it was on her. Then she thought of her fuzzy socks, and they were on her feet as well. "There you have it. You won't have to live out of boxes now, either. You'll have whatever you wish to wear when you need it."

Tabby kept staring at Punch and wondered if her mind was going too. When Edgar left her in the room with him, she got up to go to the kitchen. She didn't want to burn dinner on top of being out of her mind. She laughed just a little bit when she thought about carrying a little person around on her hand.

"Can you fly?" He lifted up and off her hand and then landed on her shoulder. "I see. And when you say that you're going to be keeping me safe, how is that going to work? I don't know that I should point this out to you, but you're much smaller than I am."

"I have an army that I can call upon to serve me and you." With a snap of his fingers, there were thousands of the little creatures in the room with them. It was Edgar who caught her again when she thought that she was going to fall forward. "I don't mean to stress you, my lady, but I know that someone who isn't used to magic or faeries needs to know that I can be trusted with keeping you safe for Lord Edgar."

While Edgar finished up their dinner, she talked to Punch and him. He didn't push her into anything, like believing that he was a dragon, but she was beginning to see that he might very well be what he said he was. When he set her a plate of pasta with red sauce in front of her, she was almost afraid to look at his face to see the disappointment there for her not believing in him.

"We have the rest of our lives to get to know one another, Tabby. Eat up, and then we'll talk more." She asked how Punch was fed. Edgar reached up and took one of the blossoms off the blooms that she'd picked up today on her way home, and the little man started to nibble on it. "He also likes sugar cubes, but he doesn't need them as often as he might like. Also, you can pour him a little juice in a saucer, and he'll really enjoy that from you."

"No meat then?" He said that they were creatures of the land and that meat wasn't in their diet. "I feel like I'm in some kind of rabbit hole if you want to know the truth."

"You're doing just fine. You're not freaking out, and we're having a nice meal while we get to know one another." He ate some of his meal before looking at her again. "I almost hate to bring this up, but you should know that you'll have a dragon on your body someplace. It'll be small but mighty. It won't get to be large until we bond. Which will be whenever you're ready." Nodding, she lowered her head so he'd not see how embarrassed she was.

"I want to see your dragon. I think that once I do that, then the other stuff will come to me easier. I know you've told me several times that you're a dragon, and while I want to believe you, it's a little harder to process than having a little man on my hand. Or a dragon on my body." He told her that they'd have to go to the other realm as there wasn't enough space here for him to shift. "Another realm? What do you mean?"

"The land of faeries and unicorns." She looked at him and knew that there was shock on her face. But instead of making fun of her, like she thought he was anyway, he took her hand into his and spoke some words that she didn't understand. When she opened her eyes, not having any idea that she'd closed them, she looked at Edgar again when he said her name. "We're here."

When he let go of her hand, she just kept staring at him. She wanted to look around, see what she could see out of the corners of her eyes, but was too afraid to. This was going to be a reality check, one that she wasn't quite ready for. She wondered if she'd ever be ready for the things that she was seeing out of the corner of her eyes.

"This is my mom and dad. You didn't get to meet them because they weren't able to come to the dinner the other night. And that's my grandmother, the previous queen." They all said hello to her, and she nodded back. "I'm going to shift now, all right? Then you'll be better off knowing what I truly am."

She looked away for only a few seconds, and when she looked back, there was a ginormous dragon sitting in the grass beside her. Well, not beside her. He was too big for her to be by him. When he put out his large…claw? She didn't know what to make of it as one of his nails was as large as she was tall. Sitting down on his palm, much like Punch did for her, she tried to make her heart beat slower as she was freaking out. Again. Just as she was ready to be taken away, the dragon closed his palm around her, and she could feel herself soaring. While she didn't know what was happening, she did know that if she fell right now, she'd be dead.

Or perhaps she was already dead. Opening her eyes again, she looked through the claws that held her to the palm and screamed. Christ, oh mighty, as her dad usually said, she was in a dragon's hand, and he was flying through the sky with her.

When she felt the landing of his great body, she held onto his claws until he opened his hand. When she got off his hand? She didn't know what to call it. She stood beside him as he laid down on the grassy knoll they were on. Looking around, she was both terrified and pissed off for how he'd treated her. There was no reason for him to take her on a flying trip when she was just wanting to see his dragon.

"What did you do to me?" He answered her by talking to her through her mind. "How can you do that? We've never exchanged blood or anything else."

"I'm your mate." She smacked him on the tip of his nose. "That really hurt. What did you do that for?"

"You were showing off. I hope you have better manners when my dad gets to see you. He's actually looking forward to it." He asked her what she was feeling right now. "Like I want to bash your head in, that's how. And I doubt very much that I hurt you. What are you fifty feet tall?"

"Close to that. I did tell you that I was a large dragon. Does your dad really want to see my dragon?" She said that he did but hoped that he'd be nicer to him. "All right, I was showing off. I'm sorry. I just wanted you to like him. He's in love with you already."

"You should have warned me what you were

going to do. What if I had fallen from your hands?" He told her that he would have died to save her. "I don't know about all that, but next time, be nicer when I want to see something. Though I don't know how anything can top your dragon. He's quite scary, isn't he?"

"He's a warrior dragon. My parents are time shifters. They go around shifting time around when there is a disaster that might well have taken out someone who is needed in the future. They'll adjust the timeline so that no one is the wiser. It's a great deal more complicated than that, but my mom can explain it to you better than I can." She asked him if she was scary, too. "She's more frightening than I am."

"And your dad. What sort of dragon is he?" He told her that he was a great and powerful vampire. "I suppose if there are going to be dragons, there are going to be all kinds of things that I've never thought of before, correct?"

"There really are unicorns too. And if you'd allow me to take you back, I'll show you all kinds of creatures that you've probably never thought were real." She told him that she really wanted to see a unicorn but nothing else this trip. "There will be other creatures around. I'm sorry about that. But they want to meet the newest bride for their dragons. It's a special day for the people and animals here to see one of their dragons find their other halves."

He took her back where he'd shifted the first time, and she was more relaxed this time. Punch was with her, and when Edgar's parents welcomed her to the family, she felt special. Someday, she'd like to come back here when she wasn't so stressed out. But when she sat down at the little table and chairs that just appeared, she thought that she really was relaxed, as relaxed as she'd ever been. She thought that she could get used to being in a place like this. If she wasn't dead or dying. Those were things that she considered when petting a unicorn while a bunch of faeries brought her tea and cookies.

Chapter 3

Tommy liked his new position at the warehouses. His dad told him that he was off the hook for any trouble that he might have caused. And he, being the asshole that he was, took it to mean that he was off the hook for anything he might do in the future too. And boy, did he have plans for the future.

One thing did bother him a bit, Tabby wasn't allowing him to be in the office without her being there. She would just turn up every time he was ready to open the safe. He knew how much was in petty cash. His dad had told him that it was off-limits to him. So did his brother at his plant. No one was very trustworthy nowadays, he thought with a laugh.

He didn't need all of it, just enough for him to flash around. He would end up taking it all, but not all at once. In fact, he didn't want to take it at all, but they were forcing him to. Without them paying him, he didn't have any recourse but to take what was right there for him to use.

Tommy didn't like the rule that his dad had made. No work, no pay. Also, he was taking too much out of his check, too. Who were FICA and SS? Taxes shouldn't be taken from someone like him. Didn't they realize that he had plans for the money they collected each week? What were they even going to do with it but put it in a bank someplace and let it grow with interest? No, he didn't like the fact that him, of all people, had to pay taxes on money that he needed. No, indeed.

"What are you up to?" Earl was another pain in his ass. Forever asking him what he was doing. If he wanted him to know, he would take out an advertisement telling him not just what he was doing hourly but what he planned during the twilight hours as well. He had his entire day mapped out, and it was no one's business. "I asked you what you were doing, Tommy? I've also told you not to be in my office when I'm not around. I know you took the petty cash already, and you need to pay it back."

"Why? Why should I have to pay it back when the sole purpose of it is to be there when you're short of funds? I suppose you've never had to have any of it, have you?" He told him that he was good with his checks and didn't run short. "Jolly good for you. I suppose you have some stashed away for a rainy day, too. I know that Tabby does. She told me that she was going to buy her a house with her money."

"She did. A lovely home that is big enough for

us to stay in when we go to visit. However, I'm betting that she's going to ignore your requests until you put the money back. When I told her what you'd done, she was pretty pissed off about it." Tommy ignored him for a moment. "Nothing to say, little brother? That's all right. You'll pay back the ten grand, or I'll have to have you arrested. It is against the law to take something that doesn't belong to you."

"You do know that my name is on the door here and in Ohio, too. Or did you forget that I'm your brother? I have needs, too, dumb ass, and I don't appreciate you telling on me like I'm five years old." Earl told him not to act like he was five then. "Dad told me that I'm forgiven of my past sins. He wants me to go out and find my own path."

"So you figure that means you can continue to steal from the hand that feeds you? Not likely. Besides, you should know that the locks have been changed on the safes, and you'll not find them easy to open again." He changed the locks? Damn it all to hell and back. That did make it more difficult for him to get cash. "Also, I've taken you off the accounts here. Dad said I was in charge, and I've made sure that every banking account knows that you're not to be able to cash any checks, nor can you withdraw any money. You don't even have a bank card that will get you money. They've all been taken care of."

"You bastard." Tommy moved towards the safe that held the checkbook and the petty cash. "I suppose you told Tabby to do the same."

"Tabby is the one that told me to do it. I think her new husband told her that would be the best way to keep someone like you out of money." Tommy asked if she was really married. "I don't know that they've really done the deed, but she's telling me that they're going to do it soon so that she can get into his accounts and him into hers. They're sharing their money."

"I suppose the next thing you're going to tell me is that this person is going to be telling her how to run Reader Fresh. Sounds like she has herself a winner there. She'll be broke within a month, I'm betting." He laughed. "She'll let a near stranger into her money but not her big brother, who has been around for a lot longer. Who is this supposed husband anyway?"

"Edgar Walsh." The name sounded familiar but not one that he could remember off the top of his head. He had better things to do than to learn and remember some jerk's name that was probably going to be sucking the business dry when it was his to do with what he wanted. "You know him, Tommy. He's with the Walsh family from Ohio. The richest people in the world, we've come to find out."

"So he's sniffing around our sister to get her money, is he? No one is that wealthy that they can't use a bit more. I no more believe that she'd marry him than I am that you're going to allow me to have some cash from the safe. You're not, are you?" He told him simply that he wasn't going to open the safe if he was in the same room with him, no. And he wasn't going to give him any cash either. "You're not very friendly, are you? You do remember that I'm related to you, and you should want to see me have the things that I want and need. Just a few thousand, Earl. No one has to know. I need to get some things taken care of. Three thousand should do it for today. You can put it back when the next check comes in."

"No." Earl sat at his desk and glared at him. "You're pathetic. You can have a job and work for your money like the rest of us do. By showing up, too. I won't pay you unless you put in a day's worth of work either."

"What are you going to be doing all day while I work hard for the money that should be mine in the first place? Playing on your computer? How many games do you have on that fucker anyway? Just give me the fucking cash, Earl." He just smiled at him. "What the fuck is wrong with me taking a bit of money from petty cash?"

"Because you don't have any intentions of paying it back, do you?" Tommy scoffed. Like he would ever think of paying back money from his family business. Like he'd been telling him, it was his name on the stationary, too, damn it. "Give it up. I'm not going to give you anything that you don't earn."

"I earned it all by being a Reader, Earl. You should be happy to turn over the money to me. Do you know why? Because I'm not forcing you to do it at gunpoint." He asked him if he really would stoop so far. "If that's what it takes, then yes, I will. Give me the money, Earl, before I have to get nasty with you."

"Get out of here." He asked him what he said. "I said for you to get out of here, and you're not to come back either. I'm going to tell Dad what you said and Tabby, too, so that she knows not to fuck around with you when you come around. Christ, I don't believe you. You're my brother, for Christ's sake. Why would you say that about threatening me? Get out of here before I call the police."

"You're regret this, Earl. I promise you you're going to regret this." He started out of the office and decided he'd give him one more chance to give over the money. "Either give it to me, or you'll be watching your back for the rest of your life. I'm not kidding you right now. Hand it over."

"Get out." Tommy left the office, but he'd be back. And when he was, he was going to kill his brother. Maybe even his sister. And that nosey kid of hers. They weren't in charge of the business. Dad was.

And he was going to see eye to eye, too."

Tommy wanted to do some serious damage to the lot when he left, but there were too many truckers there picking up their loads. Leaving the lot, he decided that he was going to tell Dad what had just happened but thought that was a bad move without backing power. He needed to find himself a gun that would show them. Getting a gun that couldn't be traced back to him or the family would be the way to go. With all the truckers around all the time, they'd surely look at them before looking at the family. His family was with the wrong sort of people, and that was what was going to get them killed.

Thinking along those lines, he decided that he also needed to find him an alibi. He'd have to think hard on it before he killed his family so that he'd not be looked at. Someplace far away. He thought about Ohio and the Walsh family. They'd be the perfect patsy's to keep him out of trouble. Maybe, he thought to himself, he'd find a way to blame it all on the newest family member.

"What was his name?" He'd remember it in time. And it would all go down just the way he wanted. No one would blame him. No one would see it coming, either. He'd come up with the perfect plan that would have him laughing for decades after it was finished.

As soon as he entered the house, he knew that

Earl hadn't wasted any time in calling his parents. Dad was pissed off. Mom would be, too, if she'd been home. Dad asked him if he'd gotten his gun yet, and Tommy had laughed.

"I was joking with him, Dad. He just can't take a joke anymore." It occurred to him that he'd just given some vital information away that could be used against him when Earl turned up dead. "What did he tell you? That I threatened him? Christ, he's my brother. I'd never do that."

"He also said you were wanting money out of the business. I told you before, Tommy, that I'll forgive you that once but not a second time. You're going to have to figure out your own way of getting cash that doesn't involve the business." Tommy sat down and looked at his dad as he sat in his comfy chair. "I didn't call the police on you the first time, but I will if so much as a dollar shows up missing. I'm not kidding, nor am I joking. I will have you arrested."

"I was joking, Dad. I promise you that I was joking around." He gave his dad the sad look that had worked every time he wanted something from the man. "I do need some cash. Earl couldn't even spare a couple hundred bucks for his little brother. I'm broke, Dad."

"He told me you wanted a few thousand." Did he say that? That's what he wanted, but he didn't remember saying it to his brother. "I don't have any cash on me, son. As I told you when I let you go from Readers, I'm not going to support you when you're well old enough to get yourself a job and hold onto it."

"What do you mean you don't have any cash? You always have a few hundred dollars on you at all times. I just need something to get me by." Dad asked him what he was getting by from. "I'm going to get me a job. I have plans, too. I got my rent paid up, and now I'm going to find me a good job that will make you proud of me."

He wanted to puke. He wasn't going to get himself a job at all unless they had one where you could make money by spending it. There was no way that he was going to be able to work a job and be the kind of person that he wanted to be. Working for a living was for suckers, and he'd not been born to money only to have it taken away from him right now. Tommy looked at his dad when he said his name.

"I asked you where you've applied. And I might have some money on me, but I'm not handing it over to you. I won't support you, Tommy. I've told you that. Get a real job and try to stand on your own two feet. Your sister did, and she's younger than you are." It was always about his sister and brother and how perfect they were. "What did you say?"

"Nothing. Well, can I stay here for a few nights

to get myself together?" Dad pointed out that his rent was caught up, so he should be able to get himself together at his own home. "Are you kicking me out of my family home, Dad? Tell me, if Earl asked, you'd allow him to stay. Or even Tabby. Right?"

"They have homes of their own and wouldn't need to get themselves together after stealing ten grand from the company. They'd never do that." Rolling his eyes, Tommy asked about Tabby being so far from home. What did he think about that? "I don't know what you're implying. She's working. Something that you seem to not understand to make herself money."

"I guess I'll never be perfect enough for you, will I father?" Dad told him that he didn't want perfect but someone that worked for what they wanted. "It's not my fault that I don't have a job. I was working for Reader when you let me go. I won't even have a reference from you, will I?"

"All I can tell someone is that you worked for me. I'll do that. Nothing more." He cursed at his father and told him that he was disappointed in him. "And I am in you as well."

~*~

Tabby was nervous about her brother coming around. Earl had called her and Dad at the same time and told them what Tommy had said to him. Earl wanted to blow it off, thinking that he'd never do that, but Tabby wasn't so sure. He'd do it, kill one of them, and then expect the other two to get in line with his thinking. He was that much of a terrible person. She went to find Edgar to see what he had to say about Tommy and him threatening them with getting a gun.

"He can't kill you. Tommy can hurt you a little, but you'll heal from that and anything else he has in mind to do to you." She asked him what he meant. "You're immortal, the same as I am. The only way to kill you is to remove your head, and I'm not sure he could do that. To remove one's head takes a very sharp blade and a lot of upper body —"

"All right. I get it. So if he shoots me in the head, somehow I'll live through that?" He told her that, yes, she was immortal. "Are my parents? My brothers? I mean, have they been given the same magic to keep them alive?"

"No. I never thought of you having that magic until just now. I can talk to my mom and have her do it for the rest of your family." She told him, not Tommy. "All right. I can have her do it to your parents and Earl. Mandy is because she's your daughter and my stepdaughter. There are other things that you can do that we've not talked about. You can reach out to my family when you need them. And if you ever need them, don't hesitate to call for them. They can and will be there for you no matter what you might think is too small for them to care about." Tabby sat down in the chair across from his desk. "Something bothering you?"

"You told me that I can change my clothing at will. You've also told me about being immortal. There is plenty more that you're not or haven't told me, right?" He nodded and said that since she was a human and him a dragon, he really didn't know what sort of magic she could get. "So I could be able to shift for all you know."

"That's right. Amy got some of my dad's vampirism, like an old vampire like he is. Then there are the things that she can do. She can hop in and out of fires without getting burnt and travel that way. I think you were told that part." She told him that Layla had told her more about it. "They'd be the ones to tell you. As they can both do that burning thing. The only way that I can tell what you got from being my mate is for you to tell me. And in order for you to know, you have to play around with it when I'm around."

"So it's sort of hit-and-miss kind of thing?" He smiled and told her that was it exactly. "I did discover one thing. I can bring things to me. It's not like they float through the air towards me, but they just pop in my hand when it's something that I can carry. Also, I've received a bag from your grandmother. She told me that it would never weigh more than it does when it's empty, but I could carry a car around in it, and it wouldn't lose its shape. That one is kind of scary if you ask me."

"Amy and the other women have one too. It comes in handy when they're shopping. You'll like that, too, I'm betting." She asked him what it was called. "An endless bag, I think, is what it's called. And so you know, if you want something from the bag, all you have to do is tell it what you're looking for, and it'll be right there for you."

"Now that's awesome." She wanted to learn more, but she was worried about her family. "Can we talk to your mom now? I don't want anything to happen to my family so long as Tommy is out there causing trouble. I don't believe my family thinks he's capable of doing anything like that, but I know better. He'll kill us without a second thought."

"We can go now if you'd like. I have some things that I need to tell my parents anyway about the contracts that they sent over today." When he stood up, she did as well. "I'm not rushing you, Tabby, but I want you to know that as soon as we bond, you'll have considerably more magic than you do now. And that's when you'll need to play around with it to know what you've gotten. It'll be there to keep you safe."

"All right. I'll start messing around with it as soon as we get back. I'm worried about my family right now." He put out his hand, and she took it. "You're very good to me, Edgar. I don't know what to think about how I feel about you, but I think that I'm falling in love with you already."

He kissed the back of her hand. "I'm already in love with you as I've ever been with anyone else. And I will love you tomorrow and all the tomorrows beyond today more than I do the day before." He pulled her into his arms and held her. "I love you so much, Tabby. You can't know how much I do without being in my heart. Now, let's go see my mom so she can help us out with keeping your family safe. I love them as well. Earl is like a brother to me, and I dearly love your parents."

His parents were at their home in this realm when they went by to see them. After explaining to them what was going on, Storm said she could do that with no problem. When she sat down at the dining room table with them, she said it was done, and just like that, all the worry that she had over her brother just rolled off her shoulders.

"Thank you so much. I owe you a great favor for keeping them safe." She said that she'd have to get with them and give them a faerie each. "I can do that. I have one, and I can't believe how much I use him for things. And he seems to love helping me, too." Alex, Edgar's father, said that they get jealous when they see one of them getting to help one of the brides. "Brides?"

"What they call the mates of our sons. They think that helping you is a huge boom, that they were specially picked to help you ladies. And if they can help you with your magic, which I'm betting that they already know what you have, then that makes them twice as proud." She asked if that was true. They'd know what she had. "I'm sure of it. They did help me with the magic that I received when I first came to be with Storm. I found them to be quite delighted to help me out with some of it, too."

"I'll get with them. How do I go about getting my family a faerie? I don't want to put anyone out, but I really want them to be safe." Storm told her that her family was as safe as she could make them and that their houses, including hers and Edgars, were fixed as well. "What do you mean fixed? And I have a lot of faeries at the house now."

"I've fixed it so that no one with ill will or ill intent can enter your homes. That would include your yard as well." She asked what the difference was. "Good question. It came to me that someone having an ill will wouldn't be able to get into your house, but if they saw you out and about, they could harm you. They cannot kill you, but they can harm you. Ill intent means that when they see you out and about, walking down the street, they could harm you then. So I've made it so that nothing untoward can harm you or your daughter, who I like, by the way, then either."

"Thank you. I'm assuming that you've given it to my family as well." Storm told her that everyone that she loves has it in their homes, but for Tommy. "Good. Thank you. I know that you don't understand why not him but I've not trusted Tommy for a very long time. He's sneaky and sort of mean. Well, I mean, he's a great deal mean, and I'm afraid of him. Or I was. He scares me to death sometimes when I see him looking at me. Like he's looking for a place to put a bullet into me that would make his day."

"I'm going to put a faerie on him as well. Not to help him but to keep an eye on him. If you don't trust him and him being your brother, then I don't trust him at all. I'll do that now." She snapped her fingers, and three of the little people came to her. After she told them what she wanted, to keep an eye on Tommy but not to engage with him, again, the fear that she had for her family rolled off her. Not completely, but enough that she wasn't as worried about them as she'd been before. "They'll be able to warn you, too, when he's coming toward you. Also, you might not have thought about this, but the more you know about your magic, the better you'll be able to keep yourself from getting harmed as well."

"Edgar and I are going to talk about that when we get back home. I never thought about what I might have." She thought of something. "Will my parents have magic too? And Earl? And Mandy? I would have to talk to them about it if they did. They're not as backwards thinking as most people their age are. They've embraced the fact that not everyone around them is human, and it's served them well."

"I've noticed that about them. When I told them I was a vampire, they didn't even blink twice. I loved it, and your father is a hoot. I like your mother in her way of just saying what she thinks, too. But your father is just funny." She told Alex that her dad was usually telling jokes when he should be serious, but again, that had served him well in the business world. "Yes, I can see that humor over getting angry would do a good job of telling people, too, that he's too smart to have the wool pulled over his eyes. He's a smart man, your father. I guess I never thought of that until just now."

"Thank you for that, Alex. You've no idea how good that makes me feel that you like him. I'll tell him, too, if you don't mind." He said it would thrill him beyond words for him to know that. "Good. I'll talk to him and my mom first. They're on their way here from home anyway. I'll call Earl as soon as I get home. I don't want him blindsided about Tommy either."

By the time she and Edgar got home, she'd spoken to Earl twice and let him know what was going on. Her parents were being picked up at the airfield by her and Edgar so that she'd tell them then.

Earl's faerie arrived and made himself known to her brother right away. He said that he did feel safer already and that he was glad someone was going to be keeping an eye on Tommy. Earl did feel bad that they had to think this way about their own family, and that was when she was told about Edgar's great-grandma and how she'd been killed by Fowler when she'd tried to kill Amy. It made her shiver when she thought of how much larger Fowler was than Edgar's dragon and that he had to kill his grannie.

Chapter 4

Tommy felt like he was being followed. But every time he thought that he'd turn, and there wouldn't be anyone behind him for blocks. The feeling made him think of his family and how they'd stoop so low as to have him followed so that they'd know every little thing that was going on in his life. Turning quickly, he thought he saw movement behind him, but it wasn't there when he looked hard. Something was going on, and he didn't care for it. Pulling out his cell phone, he called the only person he knew that could do that to him. So when his dad answered, he didn't bother with formalities but asked him straight up if he was having him followed.

"Followed? Are you doing something that would make you think that you need to be followed?" Tommy was so shocked by the question that he didn't answer him. "Don't be ridiculous, Tommy. I'm in Ohio this week for the grand opening. Why would you think that I'd have you followed? Unless, of course, like I said, you need to be."

"I'm a grown man, Dad. Why would you

be having me followed if you were? I'm not doing anything to your businesses. I'm looking for work." Dad told him how he should have come with them and to be there for the grand opening. It was going to be nice. "I'm not a part of the Reader Fresh now, am I? You've all made it perfectly clear that I'm not needed for the family's business anymore."

"You're not, and stop being so pitiful. You know why you were let go. To pursue whatever you want in the business world, isn't that right?" He didn't bother answering him because he was still hurt by the way he'd been told that he was not to come within five hundred feet of either business until he was employed. Like that was going to happen. "When you go around threatening people, you can expect to be punished by the people you threaten, Tommy. We take someone telling their brother that he's going to have to watch his back from now on very seriously. Why would you even say something like that even if you were joking?"

"Because it was a joke, and I thought he'd get a good laugh about it." He had been serious about threatening his brother and had promised him that he'd be looking over his back for a long time, but telling them that had been a colossal mistake. Now he had to watch his step around his brother because he'd told him that, and then, like a big baby, he'd told everyone around that he'd said it. It had been the police that had told him to stay away from the businesses. Christ, it was a nightmare trying to get even a hundred bucks from the offices at work. "When did he lose his sense of humor? Huh? I mean, he used to be like you, finding everything funny all the time."

"No one thinks that it was funny, Tommy. I believe you've been told that." Dad spoke to someone with him, and it was difficult for him to understand what was going on. He asked his dad if he was just too busy to talk to his son. "Why would you say that? Are you trying to cause trouble? I was talking to your brother-in-law, Edgar. You were told that your sister got married, weren't you?"

"Yeah, I heard she was married. I don't believe it, but I heard about it. Why? Why did she get married in the first place even? She only knew him for a couple of days or something, right? What's he going to do when she introduces her daughter to him." Dad told him sometimes it just hits you, and you know. "What I know is that she's going to regret marrying so quickly. What did he do, screw her a couple of times, and she insisted on marrying him? Next thing you'll be telling me is that she's going to have a kid. Wasn't one enough for her out of wedlock? Christ, wouldn't that be the straw that broke the camel's back? A kid for her to raise again while he's out draining the company you've worked so hard for."

It took him several long seconds to realize that his dad had hung up on him. He started to call him back so that he could hang up on him but decided that it wasn't worth it. But he did make a mental note that would put a black mark against his father for doing that. No one just hung up on him when he had things to say.

The hair on the back of his neck danced a little when he thought he saw a bug crawling up his leg. Christ, he danced around for ten minutes when he thought that he had a bug on him. He hated bugs worse than he did his family right now. Shivering when he didn't see it anymore, he continued on his way to his apartment to carry out some of his plans for his sister. But he could never shake that feeling that he was being followed. It was like someone was eyeing him up for trouble or something.

His apartment was clean right now because he'd had the cleaning lady come by and do her job. He didn't like others being in his place, but he'd made such a mess to his home when he'd found out that his parents had gone to Ohio again and hadn't told him that there had been no holding onto his temper. Then Dad reminded him that he had access to the shared calendar they all used, and he should have looked at it more than once a month. Dad even reminded him that he'd told him last week they were going for the grand opening in a couple of days and that he should go. Like he'd be welcomed.

He'd spoken to Tabby twice in the last two weeks. Both times, she'd told him that she didn't have time to go over the office plans with him as he'd not be getting into it anytime soon. She'd told him that she had a big safe that had her petty cash and the checkbook in it, and it was never just lying about so that he could get to it. He asked her if she didn't trust him anymore.

"I don't trust anyone with the petty cash nor the checkbooks. I write the checks, and the bank knows that. So if one comes in and it has a different signature on it other than mine, they're not to cash it." He asked her about her supposed husband. "Supposed? Why does it bother you that I'm now Tabby Walsh, Tommy? But no, he doesn't have anything to do with my business, and I don't have anything to do with his. We have enough on our mind with our own businesses and don't have time to get into someone else's."

"But you listen to him enough to keep me out of your offices, don't you?" She pointed out that he had threatened Earl. "What does that have to do with you, I wonder. I didn't threaten you. I might if you keep me out of your offices, too."

"I'm not worried about you, Tommy. I have more important things to mess with than having you tell me that you're going to get me. I'm protected very well."

He asked her by who, and she just laughed. Christ, he hated his sister then, and the more he thought about it, the more he hated her daily. "Is there something else that you wanted? I'm sort of busy right now with the grand opening in a couple of days." When he told her that he had nothing to say to her, she hung up on him. It was getting to be bad when they were all just hanging up on him for no reason.

He had plans, and so far, he'd not been able to go through any of them when he wanted them over with. Tommy had taken out insurance on his family by way of the internet, and the first payment was due in a couple of weeks. He'd been sent a bill for them, and now all he had to do was kill them off and collect before he made the first payment. Excited about having read about that on the internet on how much a person could make by taking out a policy on someone before you killed them. Tommy had been thinking of making a practice run by taking one out on one of his buddies to see how quickly he got his money. All in the name of practice makes perfect, he thought.

The article that he'd read had said the turnaround was only a few weeks. Well, that could be too many for him as he needed money now. While he'd paid up his rent and his phone, he didn't have much in the way of spending money now, and that was irritating him something awful. It was all Tabby's fault, too. Her and that damned husband of hers.

Just as he was making himself something to eat, he sorted through his mail. There, in the pile of overdue notices, he found the paperwork for Tabby's insurance policy. Pulling it out of the envelope and tossing it away, he looked at the numbers on the thing and thought he should have done this a long time ago. Taking out policies on people that he'd had to kill off. It had only been three, but that would have netted him three million bucks by now, and that wasn't anything to sneeze about. He picked up the bill to the thing and read it over. It was then that he saw that the policy was null and void until he had made the first payment on it.

"Well, mother fuck. That's fucking not going to work out too well for me, now is it?" Tommy had been talking to himself since he'd been about eight years old when he noticed that other people weren't as smart as he was. Especially his family. Also, he got the answers that he wanted as well when he answered his own questions.

Eating leftovers was all right, he supposed when it was pizza, but anything else was just crap. As he was finishing off his meal, he decided that it was way past time for him to get what he wanted from the office of Reader Fresh. His brother had to come through for him, or all this hard work was going to be for nothing.

Picking up his cell, he called Earl and had to wait for several rings to go to voicemail. He didn't leave a message but did hang up. Where was he that he couldn't answer his phone? He did wonder if he'd gone to the grand opening but didn't know for sure. It would be just like them to leave him by himself while they were off having fun.

Calling Tabby, he got the same voicemail recording. That she wasn't near her phone and couldn't take his call. There was something about contacting Edgar if it was an emergency, but since she didn't leave any number for him, he didn't have any way to call him back. Just as he was going to toss his phone across the room, it rang with an unknown number.

"What the hell do you want, mother fucker? I don't have time to talk to your unimportant self." The laughter pissed him off more. "I'm hanging up now, and you'd better—"

"It's Edgar Walsh. You called your sister's phone, and I thought that I'd help her out by asking what you need in the way of help." He told him that he wanted to talk to Tabby. "Well, that's not going to happen today. She's talking to people who might want to do business with her new opening of Reader Fresh. Now, is there anything that I can help you with right now?"

"Are you now fielding calls for her? Like I care,

but I wanted to talk to her. It's important that I get her to call me back within ten minutes. I'm not fucking around with her calling me back at her convenience. I need her now." He said that he could help him or he'd be shit out of luck for her calling him back. "You gonna give me money on behalf of my sister then? I want five grand so that I can pay off some things I have."

"You mean like the insurance policies that you've taken out on your family? I'm sorry, but I won't help you with that. I'll help you with your phone bill. I figure you need it to get prospective jobs to call you back. Though I don't think that's ever going to happen since you've never so much as applied to any place that I know of." Tommy couldn't speak. All he heard was policies, and his world just stopped moving. He asked him what he was talking about but feared it was too late now to think he was getting away with anything. "The four one million dollar policies that you took out on your family. I did wonder about why you didn't take one out on your mom, but I figured you'd get around to it sooner or later. You're sort of lazy when it comes to you following through on shit, aren't you?"

"What the hell do you think you know about me? My family been telling lies on me? That's the only way that you'd know anything about me since I've never met you." He was pissed off now that he had time to think about it. How he found out was beyond him, but he wasn't going to confirm nor deny whatever the man thought was going on. "You just stay the fuck away from my sister and the rest of my family. And don't be spreading lies either, or you'll be the next one to get on my hit list."

"I'm not worried about you at all, Thomas James Reader. I've gotten about all the information on you as one could get on a lazy, cheap fuck. And that's what you are." The man laughed, and it made his hair dance on his neck and arms again. "Stay away from your family, Tommy boy, or the next time you have to look around to see who is following you, you might well see that you've pissed off a dragon, and he'll have you for a snack. Do you understand me, jackass? I'm coming for you, and you'd better be ready when I do."

He had no idea how long he held the phone to his ear after the man hung up. Tommy didn't know what else he might have said either after he commented on him being watched. The man knew too much. Looking around the room, he put his cell phone back on the table with a shaky hand and backed away from it. The man knew too much. And Tommy couldn't figure out how he'd gotten the information that he had. The man knew entirely too much information about him, and it scared him to death.

It was nearly dark when he left his apartment again. He'd sat around the place for the last few hours trying his best to figure out what had happened that Walsh found out about his working on killing off his family. Going back through his mail, he found the other three policies that were for his niece, brother, and father, and they said the same thing. Without a payment on the policies, there would be no payout. And something about the policies and rules he'd not known about was that if there was a claim on the policies within ninety days of being taken out, the police would be notified of wrongdoings on his part. People, it seemed to him, were out to get him.

Tonight, he was picking up a gun. He'd traded his PlayStation gaming set for it, and he thought that he was getting the best deal. It had been months since he'd played on the game and had been about to toss it in the trash. Lucky for him, the guy had said he'd take something that he had out in trade.

The deal was for them to meet at the new chicken place on MacIntyre. Tommy was early by thirty minutes but was surprised by the three men in police uniforms who were at the place. They were talking to a man who looked like the person he was to meet.

A man in a yellow sweatshirt and dark jeans with him having bright yellow hair. Looking at his phone on the arrangements that he'd made, it did indeed say that they were to meet at the right place. He'd nearly been screwed by it being a scam from the police. He'd said this before. People weren't all that trusting nowadays. Walking back to his apartment to get rid of his gaming system, he tried to think how they'd known about him meeting Mr. Gunz when he was supposed to.

As soon as he was inside, he closed all his curtains and turned off all his lights. He'd not given Mr. Gunz his address, but now that he thought about it, the man was persistent on getting something from him, like a name or his home address. Sitting on his couch in the dark, Tommy didn't know what to do now.

The laughter woke him up. Tommy hadn't meant to fall asleep, but now that he was awake, he had to look around his place for whoever was in there with him. The laughter continued until he heard a small voice talking to him. It told him that his name was Fred and that he was sent to watch over him.

"Who sent you?" Fred said that he should be able to guess that. "I don't know who you're talking about. I don't know people that would send out someone to keep an eye on me."

"Sure, and you do, Mr. Tommy. My lord Edgar sent me to you to keep an eye on you for trouble. I've been told that I can talk to you now. I'm not supposed to let you see me, they being afraid that you'd try and harm me somehow. But that's all right with me.

I've been given a great gift to watch over one such as yourself." He told him to show himself, or he'd not believe him. "Well, now that's a lie, isn't it? You're talking to me, so you know you have to believe in me. Nah, I'll not show myself to you. You being the kind of man that you are. And I called the police on you when you went looking for a gun. Even set it up so that Mr. Gunz — what a clever name that is — was a police officer to catch you. Now, all I have to do is wait for you to mess up again. Next time, they'll catch you for sure."

"I'll pay you double what Edgar is — that's my sister's supposed husband — isn't it? He's paying you something to lie to my family about me." Fred said that there were no lies from him. That he'd taken out the policy and that he was trying for a gun to kill them with. Besides, he didn't have any money to double anything for him. "I do, too, have money. Or I will as soon as I can get into the offices. I'll go there now and show you how easy it is for someone like me to get money whenever I want it."

"You can go there, but you'll never get inside the place. Lady Tabby's place, either. It's been worth it to miss out on all the pretties that she has been giving away at the grandiose opening of her new, fresh place. You know, I've never thought that it would be such a big deal to eat and to deal with fresh stuff before. That's all I eat is fresh. I know you don't like anything green on your plate, and you'll have some health issues, more than you have now for not taking fresh vegetables and other good things into your diet." Tommy decided that he wasn't going to talk to the person anymore. "Ah well, that's all right with me if you don't want to talk to me. I've been given special powers that allow me to read your mind for trouble. Speaking to me or not, it makes little difference to me. I'll get the information that is needed to keep the other family safe."

"You stay the hell out of my mind." He felt the little nudge to his mind and put his hands over his head so nothing could be put into it. That was the only way that he knew of that someone could probe his mind. "I want you to show yourself to me, or I'm going to call the police."

The laughter again. "You go on telling them that someone is talking to you and getting into your mind and see what that gets you. More than likely, you'll be at the funny farm with a lot of other people who think I'm not real." He asked him what he was. "Faerie. A blue one, too."

That made him laugh. A faerie, a blue faerie? There wasn't any such thing as a faerie, much less a blue one. As he started to tell him how he'd come to be, someone knocked on his door. Going to get it, he was surprised and displeased to find the police there.

Tommy told him that he was talking to a faerie and he'd have to wait for whatever he wanted.

"A faerie? Is that right? You got little people running around here that only you can see, sir?" Tommy asked the cop what he was talking about. "Little people are the faeries, Mr. Reader. But that's not what I'm here for. I'm here because you were talking to a person by the handle of Mr. Gunz. You had an appointment with him an hour ago, and you didn't show up. I'm here to tell you that we've been watching you and know that you're out looking for a gun. I don't suppose you'd tell me what it is you plan to do with said gun, would you?"

"I don't know what it is you're talking about." He asked why his PlayStation was lying in the bag on the floor. "That's none of your business, now is it?"

He felt pretty good about his answer to the cop about his toys. The man was barking up the wrong tree if he thought that he was going to just confess to having him tell him what he'd been up to. Here he thought that cops were supposed to be smart, and he couldn't believe how stupid this guy was being. Like Tommy was some dumbass that would actually confess to getting a gun for his toys. Stupid man wasn't going to get him to do anything where he'd be in trouble. He'd just have to find another way to get himself a gun and not have the police following him around to get himself in trouble.

"He'll catch you, Mr. Tommy, because I'm going to be telling him all your plans when you have one. You're not all that smart, you know. Dumber than a brownie that's been out of the bud too long. They get to be a little silly when they think that they can work in the big people world." He put both his hands on his head when Fred started talking again. "Won't do you a bit of good doing that. It just makes you look silly. A man holding his head like you're doing can only reflect badly on someone who already thinks there is something off about you."

"Is there something bothering you, Tommy? Something that I can help you with?" He said that the faerie was talking to him about his plans. "Oh, so he's going to know them too. You tell him that if he finds out that you're up to no good, he can surely call me. If that's possible anyway. Yes, I'll take the information to keep your family safe."

Tommy didn't want to talk to anyone anymore and asked the officer if he had any more questions. When he said that he didn't, he closed the door on him and turned to look around the room. There wasn't anyone around him. Not a person, little or big, was in the room with him. But the voice was still there, telling him that he knew now who to talk to in the station house if he was going to continue on the same path that he was on now.

"Just leave me alone, will you? I have nothing to say to you. And stay out of my thoughts; they're mine, and I won't have you getting me in trouble with them." He thought of what the cop had said, he'd given him his name and email address for the little person, if there was a little person around to call him when he knew what Tommy had been up to. "You're messing with the wrong guy, Fred. I'm telling you right now that you're messing with the wrong man when you mess with me. I'll get you. You can be assured of that."

For the rest of the evening and into the early hours of the next morning, Fred told him every thought that went through his head. He even told him that the meds he took for his head aching weren't going to stop him. Tommy was ready to call it all off, but he had a feeling that was just what they wanted. For him to call off the killing of his family, and he wasn't that far gone as yet.

~*~

Edgar kept an eye on the Reader family. Mostly Tabby, but he watched the other four as well. He was glad that they were taking it so well that they had a faerie around them all the time. In fact, he'd been told by the little faerie that was with Sheppard that he had found out that his little person could play a good game of chess, and the two of them were doing that every evening.

Gina was also having a good time with her little man. He was helping her in the garden, knowing which one of the things in her garden were weeds, flowers, or herbs. She'd been having such a wonderful time with him that Crockery had asked if he could have a couple of seeds from the palace so that she could see what they grew in the gardens there. He did wonder if Earl and his little faerie were a good match when he saw him talking to him about the fresh items and how she could help with keeping them fresh for longer so long as he approved it. It was working out well better than he thought. Edgar was very excited.

"You look very happy. What have you been up to?" He told Gina, Sheppard's wife, that he'd been keeping an eye on everyone for them. "I know that you have been Edgar, and you've no idea how much that means to me. I believe that I've enjoyed my day much more simply because I feel like you've taken a great burden from our shoulders. I know that Tabby is happy, too."

"It's good to be appreciated in times like this, but I want to make sure that the four of you are around for a good long time for Tabby." She nodded, then turned and asked him why they were telling people they were married. "It's been filed in the courthouse that we have been so that no one will be the wiser about us only living together. My mom is happy for that, too.

But that doesn't mean that we won't be married some other time if Tabby wants to. Or Mandy wants us to. It's just now, with everything going on, I can keep her safe and not have to worry about Tommy or whatever he's up to."

"Is he up to something?" He simply nodded. "I want to ask you what he's been doing, but I have a feeling that you'd tell me straight up and without any kind of niceties. Don't get me wrong, I love you for that, but I'm having—just tell me what he's been doing while we're all here."

"He's tried to purchase a gun today." Edgar grabbed her hand when she looked as if she was going to fall backwards. "I'll learn to give you information the next time I give you something."

"No, don't do that. It just occurred to me that he's going to try and kill us all for money." He held onto her when she swayed a little bit. "I'm all right now, young man, and I'm glad that you told me. I kept telling myself that he'd not be like that, not even to his own mother, but I know better now, and it'll make me keep an eye out for him, too. I won't be as trusting anymore about what he says to me, either. I don't like this feeling that my son is such a monster, but I know in my heart and mind that he is. Thank you for that."

"I'm here for you anytime. Can you take any more news, or have you had enough for now? I can and will tell the others about what he's up to, but you asked me, and I'll do anything within my power to make sure that you are all right." She said that she knew that, too, for some reason. Then she told him to never not tell her something because he thought she couldn't handle it. "Good. He's taken out insurance policies on Tabby, Mandy, Earl, and your husband. He didn't know that they were not going to be cashed out if he'd not paid on them. Tommy was going to take the one out on you when he got some more cash from the other four accounts. Tommy is now trying to deal with his faerie talking to him all the time and telling him that his ideas aren't going to work from now on."

"How much was he expecting to get from killing us all off?" He told her. "Four million dollars. I guess I thought that it would be for more. He's never been a good planner." She put her hand over her mouth when she spoke. "I made that sound like I'm disappointed in him for only taking out a million dollars on us. My goodness, what you must think about me."

"I think that you're a good woman who has been dealt a shitty hand in her son. I don't know yet why he thinks he's deserving of the money or killing you all off, but I will tell you that he's not very smart in thinking that he can outwit me. I've dealt with his kind all my life, and I know how to make the system work for me and you." She nodded again, and he could see the tears as they flowed down her cheeks. "If Tabby sees that I've made you cry, she's not going to be happy with me. Especially when I tell her about your son."

"I'll talk to her." Gina started away but turned back to him. "I'll tell my husband about this if you'd not mind. I don't want him to know today, right now anyway. They're all having such a good time that I don't want to ruin this for them. I should have waited, too. That's on me, not you. But like I said, Edgar, if I need to know something, I want you to tell me right away. I can't fight what I don't know about."

"I understand, and I will do that for you." When she stepped away from him, Edgar reached out to his entire family to let them know what was going on. He told them everything, including Tommy going to trade his system for a gun and how that had turned out. Edgar also told them how Fred was working on the man to keep him off guard. "Fred is talking to him, but he's not allowed to show himself to him. I believe that it would be certain death for the little man."

"You can be sure of that, I'm afraid." He told his dad that there were several that were working on Tommy and that he didn't want any of them harmed. "You're a good man, son. I don't know that I would have thought of everything that you have to keep your mate safe. She sure is having a wonderful time tonight, don't you think?"

"I think she's the most beautiful creature ever created, and I can't believe that she's all mine. I love her so much, Dad, that I'm almost disbelieving about how I feel about her." Dad chuckled, and it made him smile. "I'm going to go and find her and talk to her about tomorrow. She's not going to open to the public anymore, but she has drivers coming in and loading up. I think she's just excited to have the place open for business."

"I'm proud of you both right now." He thanked his dad for what he said and found it difficult for him to contain his own tears. His father was the best. Both his parents were. "You be a good son and keep an eye on your new little family, and we'll watch your back. Don't ever think that I don't have your back, son. I'd die if anything were to happen to any of you."

"I feel the same way about you and Mom." Finding Tabby proved to be a little difficult, but once he did, he couldn't believe how much she was glowing with happiness. "How about I take you away from all this, and we get some real food to eat? I understand why you wanted to have fresh out with this thing, but I'm starving for real food and think you might be as well."

"I could easily eat a horse right now." She eyed him kind of side-eyed. "You don't eat those too often, do you?"

"I think that it's been decades since I wanted horse meat. And even then, I think my dragon only ate a small portion." She looked shocked at him. "I'm kidding, honey. I swear that the only time I've eaten horse was when I was fighting a war between castles, and that was all there was for any of us to eat."

"I don't want to know." He said he could give her that, no information. "Thank you. Now, tell me what has made my mom so upset. I saw the two of you talking. It's about Tommy, isn't it? Tell me, please. I've had a really good day, and I need to know that he's not around here and going to fuck things up for us."

He told her everything, including what his dad said about keeping the faeries safe. Once she had all the information that he had to give her, she wandered away from him. He let her go because it was a lot to digest right now, particularly about her own brother. When she came back to him, she hugged him tightly and thanked him. It was all he could do not to tell her she'd be stronger still if she bonded with him—that worried him enough—but he wasn't going to pressure her into anything she didn't want to have happen. She was his mate, and he'd do anything in the world to not have to keep her safe from her own brother. Tommy would be dead right now if he'd been allowed to kill the younger man as soon as he heard what he was up to.

Chapter 5

Tabby wanted a burger and fries. Mandy had gone home with her parents again and was spending the night there. The only place to get them was at the small ice cream shop not far from where the plant was. She stood in line in her business suit and smiled at the kids, teenagers who were there getting their nightly quota of soda and frozen delights.

"I just thought of something." She turned to Edgar as he stood in line behind her. "You'll never gain any weight now either, with the exception of when you're carrying our children. If you want any."

"I do. Not right away, I don't think. I've only just got my business up and going, and I don't want to take away from that right away. Because when we have children, I want to be able to devote all my time to them and not work. Is that all right? Mandy has been asking too if we'll have her a brother or sister. I think she'll be a good helper to us." He kissed her on the nose, and she smiled at him. "Are you getting out of a conversation, or is that the way you're telling me yes, it's all right?"

"It's more than all right with me that you want to spend time with our children. I'm thinking perhaps we should have a dozen or so, but that'll be up to you." She laughed when he shut her mouth for her. "I'm joking. We'll have as many children as you wish and no more. I'm just happy to have you in my life. I could care less about anything that tries to take us apart."

After putting in her order for dinner, Edgar ordered the same thing but doubled his order. He'd not been kidding when he said that he was hungry. She wondered if he'd eat like that all the time and was glad that they had money or she'd — Tabby thought of feeding their children and thought of all the calories they'd have as being part dragon. She asked him about that.

"Yes, they'll eat a great deal when they're old enough to go out on their own to find dinner. However, we'll teach them how to be discreet about how much they eat at one place. It's why, as a family, we never go to all-you-can-eat places. We'd put them out of business if we were all to get our fill." She laughed, thinking about one of them going up to a buffet and taking out the tray of fried chicken as their starter meal. She turned to look at him when he said her name. "They'll be dragons, too. Because of us being so magical, all of our children will be dragons when they're born."

"I did wonder about that. Emma was telling me

that she will only carry the hatchling for five months, and then it will be an egg for them to watch over for another six months before it will be born. She's both excited and terrified at the same time to be having a dragon, the first of many, she told me." Picking up their food, they went to sit on one of the picnic tables that were provided for people having dinner. "How many eggs do you have at one time? I'm sure they're large when they come."

"The eggs will be small for her to birth. Then, as the dragon grows within it, the egg will accommodate itself for them. By the time they're ready to be hatched, they'll be about the size of a nine-month-old baby. It will also be a human-looking baby until it reaches the age of maturity. That's about twenty-five." She asked if they could shift before that. "No. They'll know that they're dragons but won't be their true self until they reach that age. It's safer for them that way. Not just for the hatchling but for all of us. Can you imagine a teenage dragon having a temper tantrum? It would be a disaster for everyone around them."

They both laughed, and she finished her burger and played around with her fries, thinking about her brother Tommy. He'd not always been like he is now, she wondered. The longer she sat there thinking about him, the more she realized that he'd always been somewhat of a prick to everyone that was around him.

"When I was ten and him fourteen, Tommy ruined my birthday cake. Mom had gotten me what I wanted, and that was just a plain white cake with my name on it. No roses or any of that fancy work they usually put on the cakes. I couldn't stand those flowers—too sweet for me. But Tommy wanted to have chocolate cake. Which I don't like chocolate at all. While we were in the yard having a celebration, Tommy was in the house covering my cake with cocoa powder, like an inch thick of it all over the cake and any presents that were around too." Edgar said that he was a jerk. "You've no idea. And when he was punished for his actions, Mom said that the next week, she'd get me another cake, and we'd celebrate without him. I think that was when he ended up in military school and out of our house by then. He didn't do so well there either, just so you know."

"No, I don't imagine that he would. Not with someone telling him what to do every day." By the time Edgar had finished his meal, she was ready to go home. "I can do that for you. But remember, we have plans for in the afternoon tomorrow. You have orders going out in the morning, and the rest of the day is for us. After that, I'm assuming that you'll be too busy for your poor old husband."

She smacked him on the arm and laughed. "I'll be too busy for a lot of things, but not you nor Mandy.

You two are going to be first and foremost in my life from now on. Even if I have to hire someone to come in and take over for me sometimes. I was talking to Mom, and she said that I need to hire someone like that anyway so that I'm not working myself to death."

"I have my brothers to take over for me when I need some time off. Sidney is really good at contracts, too, and can usually take over for me at a moment's notice. Dyson too. He doesn't care for it as much as Sidney and I do, but he'll help me out when I ask." She nodded, thinking more and more about getting a person in who could take over for her, even if it was only a day or two a week. Since they were open every day to get products out, she wasn't going to burn herself out by being there all the time. "Are you all right?"

"Yes, I was thinking about how many hours I'd be putting in if I didn't find someone to work for me a couple of days a week. Dad used to do that, work every day until Mom put her foot down. He was really stressed out a lot of the time, and it was affecting his health." Tabby told Edgar about the heart attack scare they had with her dad and how he'd gotten out of the business altogether and turned it over to her and Earl. "He always covered for us when he saw we were beginning to stress out, but he never went back for more than a day or two a month. He was scared when the doctor told him that he was overweight and his heart was working too hard to sustain the kind of abuse that he was putting it through. He lost weight, started walking around the block every day, and was a better man for it. I was terrified myself when I was told what the doctor had told him."

"I don't blame you one bit. I don't know what I'd do without my parents around. Mom and Dad have been there for us our entire life. Even with them living in the other realm, they still make time to see us. And we get together once a week if we can to have a meal together. It's at that time we catch up on our lives and reconnect with each other." Edgar held her hand as they walked back to his car. "Has my mom talked to you about taking over the faerie gardens around the town? She said that she thought you'd be perfect for the job."

"Yes, she did. I only need to make sure that they're in good shape. I don't know how they'd be in better shape with me watching over them. The faeries take really good care of them already." She laughed a little. "The hanging baskets, from what I was told, make a great hiding place for them when they're not working around the gardens. I guess they're too high for humans to look into, and they have a wonderful time spying on the humans. They're so fascinated by us, aren't they?"

"Yes. They love the women's colorful hairstyles. I think that's why they started dying their own hair. Of course, they can only dye it with fruits and vegetables, so it doesn't last all that long, but they do have a blast doing it to themselves. Also jewelry. They love all things sparkly." Edgar started laughing when he thought of something. "One year for Christmas, for a joke, my dad gave a bottle of glitter to one of his faeries. I don't need to tell you how well that went over. And it was everywhere. Dad said they were sprinkling it all over themselves and then flying around dropping it on things around the house like that faerie in that Disney movie. Needless to say, he never did that again. I think to this day there is still multicolor glitter around the house that Fowler lives in, and occasionally, you'll find a small bit of it on my dad's clothing."

"Now I'm going to be looking for it on him." They both laughed as they drove to her home. "Will you stay tonight? I mean, not in my bed yet, but I'd like to have you close to me when I go to bed."

"I'd be honored to stay with you. How many bedrooms do you have open right now? I know that you're parents and brother are staying." She told him about her parents. "Well, that was nice of them to fill out the room that they'll be using. Earl, too, I suppose." She nodded. "That's wonderful for you. I love that they'll have their own rooms when they come to visit us."

"Me too. I know it's a lot to ask of you, but I just want you near me." Edgar told her that it wouldn't be any trouble for him. He only had a condo to go home to. "Thank you. I know that it seems silly, but I feel safer with you around."

"That's not silly at all. I love being close to you so that we can all three be safer. And so you know, Tommy is still in Tennessee and not anywhere near here. He's not been to the other plant either." She asked if the faerie was safe. "Yes, he's having too much fun driving him a little over the edge, but that's all right, too. Tommy isn't happy that nothing is going right for him. Which I think is just perfect for him. Keep him guessing about what's going on, and that'll make him make mistakes. Serious ones that will get him caught."

"I don't want him hurt, not really, but I want him to be out of our hair for a while. Do you think that if he were to be able to go to jail, they'd straighten him out?" He told her that he didn't know anyone in the system, so he couldn't tell her what would happen to him. "Probably not. He'll be worse more than anything else. If he makes it there. I don't see him using his time there to reflect on what he's done to get him there. Oh damn him and being the way that he is."

"Just keep telling yourself that you're going to be all right, and so will your family. He can't kill you, and that's his plan." Tabby told him that she was fine with that too, that he might well be killed in trying to kill them off. "He can hurt you but not kill you. Hurts will heal, but dead will not."

"Good point. But still, he's my brother, and I do love him. But I don't like him all that much. Does that make sense?" He told her that it did. "I knew you'd understand about him. I really do love him with all my heart, but I don't like what he's become. Not at all. He's going to try and murder us all for money. Can you believe that? I can't. It doesn't seem real to me."

After showing him to the room that he was going to use, he asked her for a good night kiss. As much as she wanted to give him all of herself, she knew that her parents and brother could come into the hall at any moment. So with a very chaste kiss, he told her he'd see her in the morning and if she needed him to just yell. He'd be her knight in shining armor.

Going to her own room, she was stopped by her dad. Mom had told him what was going on with Tommy, and he wanted to make sure that she had all the information that she needed. It broke her heart to see her dad so upset, but she was glad too that they were all on the same page when it came to him. No one wanted him dead, but they did want him to pay for the threats he was making. That was not only dangerous but also very stressful. She wanted tomorrow to be better and hoped that it would be.

Getting into her bed, she didn't think she'd sleep all that well. There was just too much on her mind to allow herself to relax enough to go to sleep. But almost as soon as her head hit her pillow, she could feel herself drifting off to sleep. Not sleeping the night before all that well was probably a big factor in that, and she was exhausted. Tomorrow was going to be better, she kept telling herself, and she was going to make sure of it.

~*~

Tommy was standing outside the warehouse when the lights suddenly came on. He didn't know what was going on, but he hid behind some of the large crates that food came in on and waited. It wasn't until he saw the men who worked for his brother messing around with the trucks that he realized that it was going to be opening up today. As far as he knew, his stupid brother hadn't shown up as yet. And he called him a lazy fuck.

"No, he hasn't. It's you that are the lazy fuck. I don't usually curse like that, but that's what you are." The being again. He finally got it to shut up when he went to sleep. He didn't know if the creature ever slept, but he was exhausted from dealing with shit all day that he decided he'd lock himself in his bedroom and get some sleep. Fat lot of good it had done him to lock the door. He came right into the room and started talking again. "Did you know that your sister is a good person? She is. Right nice to others like me, too. Why her own faerie is the envy of all the other faeries, too. She gives him fresh flowers to eat every day."

"I don't care." He didn't either. "I'm not going to be nice to you nor feed you while you're here busting my chops. Go to hell."

Pulling the pillow up and over his head, he was finally able to drown him out. As soon as he closed his eyes, he was asleep and feeling pretty relaxed enough to not be bothered by the strange person.

Now, here he was the next morning at the plant. All he had to do was get inside the offices, figure out where his brother would have written down the combination to the safe, and get out the money and a few checks to cash when he got low again. He should have done that the first time, gotten himself some other means to get cash, but now that he knew, he was going to take about a dozen of them and get what he wanted done. He only needed a gun to kill off his sister, and he'd be sitting pretty.

He'd decided sometime in the middle of the night to kill Tabby off first. She, being the youngest, wouldn't be missed as much as Earl would, as he was the oldest and having been around for a while longer than even him. He could use the money that he was going to get from his brother's plant to pay off her insurance policy and have the million that she'd bring in.

This was a smarter plan than killing them all off at the same time. He could balance out his cash coming in by killing the others every few months. Tommy didn't know what he'd do after all his family was gone, but he was a smart man and would figure out something to keep the cash flowing.

He did wonder if he'd be caught killing them off. He decided that he was going to have to be injured himself for anyone to believe that he wasn't part of the deaths of his family. He didn't know why they'd not believe him when he told them that he'd not been in on their deaths. He was a great liar and could keep them guessing for a long—

"Tommy, what are you doing here?" He screamed a little when his brother spoke to him from behind. He nearly wet himself too when he saw that he wasn't alone but with a couple of police too. "I thought you were told to stay away from the plant here by five hundred feet. You're on the property now."

"Where is Mom and Dad?" He said that they were at their house, unpacking. "Yeah, did you have a good time without me? I would have liked to have gone there, too."

"We did have a great time because you weren't there. I never realized how stressful you make things until I was away from you." He told him he was rude.

"Rude or not, we had a great time, and Tabby was able to generate a lot of new business for her plant. You should have seen her. She was nearly glowing with love, too, for her husband. I hope I can find someone like that to love me when I'm ready."

"That's disgusting. Why would you want a person to love you like that? It's nasty the way that she hangs on his every word, too. Like nothing that I say to her matters. Disgusting." Shaking his head, he started for the plant. "Where are you going, Earl? I'm not finished speaking to you yet. Don't walk away from me. It's not right that you think I'm going to be okay with you doing that."

"I have work to do. And shouldn't you be out finding a job by now? I'd think that you'd find something for yourself. You've been unemployed from here for a few weeks now." He told Earl that it was none of his business what he was up to. "Just so long as you don't come into the plant asking for a handout, I don't really care what you're up to anymore."

"I need some cash. I spoke with Dad, and he said it was all right if you were to give me some of the petty cash." He heard Fred tell him that he was a liar again. "Shut up. I'm not talking to you." That had the cops with his brother laugh like he was a madman talking to himself. "Go away, why don't you? You have to have more to do than to hang out around here."

"We're to watch things when you're around. We wouldn't want you to get into any trouble again, now would we? I heard about Mr. Gunz and your system being traded for a gun. Why didn't you go through with it? It sure would have saved us a bunch of time in trying to watch over you all the time. Don't you think?"

"You don't want to know what I think. I want you to go away so that I can talk to my brother." The other cop said that he wasn't getting any cash from the place. "Fat lot, you know about it. My dad said I could have some cash so I can get me something to eat. Not that it's any of your business."

"Everything about you is our business right now, Tommy boy." That was the second time in two days that someone had called him that. He didn't like it anymore now than he did yesterday. "You find yourself a gun yet? I'm thinking that it's going to be a bit harder for you to find one now that we're watching you all the time. Yes, sir, I think we might just enjoy watching over you for the rest of your life around here."

When he decided that he'd had enough of the good old idiots talking to him, he realized that Earl had disappeared. Walking toward the building, he was about three feet from the door when he was blocked. He didn't understand how he was blocked, but he couldn't take another step forward, only backward. Tommy couldn't even reach out his hand to try and grab the doorknob to get in. He asked Fred what was going on.

"I would imagine that the good queen has put some magic around the place. If you have ill will in your heart or mind, then you'll not be able to enter. That's right smart of her to do that to you. Right smart indeed. I would imagine, too, that it's all around their houses. Goodness, that queen is surely smart for putting that sort of magic around the place. Don't you think so?" He said that he didn't think it was smart at all. And how was he supposed to talk to his family if he was blocked? "I'd say that you're going to have to change your ways if that's something you could do. I'm kinda leaning toward you not being able to do anything like that. You being nice isn't something that you know how to do anymore."

"So in order to get past this magic, all I have to do is be nice and think nice things. I can do that." He tried several more times, and it did him little good. "This is just stupid. I'm calling my brother and having him come out here and get this taken care of. I'm part of this family, too, you know. I shouldn't be blocked out of anything that has the Reader name on it. Mother fuck."

Tommy pulled out his cell phone and tried to

make it work. In a fit of rage last night, after ordering a pizza and them not giving it to him when he didn't have any money until later had pissed him off something terrible. He'd tossed the phone across the room and heard it shatter about the same time he realized that he wouldn't have any kind of phone because he didn't have the money to get himself one. Finally, after several tries and a lot of curse words, he got it to call Earl.

"I'm needing you to come out here and move this ridiculous curse off the building." He couldn't believe that he'd been reduced to believing in magic to get things done his way. "It won't allow me to come into the plant, and I need to talk to you about something."

"I've spoken to Dad, and he said that he'd not given you permission to get any cash out of me. Also, he said to tell you that if you want money, then to get a job. None of us are going to be funding your little projects anymore. Did you really take out a million-dollar policy on me so you could collect on it when I'm dead?" He asked him where he'd gotten that information, and he just knew he was going to say Walsh had told him. And he did. "Edgar said that you'd taken out one on all of us but for Mom. That's pretty shitty, don't you think so? I mean, how were you going to pay for it if you don't have a job or money right now? I'm assuming you read the fine print on them. You have the policy less than ninety days before the person is dead, then they contact the police. That means that you'd have to make three payments on it before you could kill me off. Which, by the way, isn't going to happen."

"You don't think I can kill you, or you don't believe that I'd kill you, my brother?" He said neither one was going to work. "Oh, but I believe that you're wrong about that, big brother. I'm very handy with a gun."

He looked around when he remembered the police. But they were talking to some of the truckers that were in the lot. Truckers were a dirty lot, and he would bet that by the end of the day, his family wouldn't have any truckers working for them as the police would find out their plans of ripping them off.

"You're not a nice person, are you? I mean, I knew that since you were little, but you've gotten worse with age. I don't like you very much, Tommy." Tommy looked at Earl when he spoke. "Yes, I'm talking about you and how wrong I've been about you going through a phase in your life. But you're worse than you were as a child even."

"Like I care what you feel about me. When you're dead, and you will be, I promise you that, when you're dead and buried, I'm still going to be here running this place like I should have been doing from the beginning.

You were never smart enough to run a multimillion-dollar business." Earl grinned and told him that it was a multibillion-dollar business, not million. "Whatever you have to tell yourself, you pansy. There is no way that Dad would allow you to run this place if it was indeed a multibillion-dollar business. You're just too stupid."

Earl laughed, but it wasn't friendly like he normally would expect from his family. But hard and harsh. When he straightened his tie and looked at him up and down, Tommy felt less than worthy of himself for some reason.

"I might be stupid to you, but I am running this business, and Tabby is going to be making more at her plant. See that I'm right on that." He laughed again and started to turn away before he looked at him again. "You're not worth me standing out here and wasting my breath on. You won't get into the plant ever, and I find myself thrilled about that. Good luck with your endeavors, Tommy. I hope you get what you deserve."

When he walked away from him, Tommy saw red. Christ, what was with his family these days? Thinking that he was going to be all right with them getting the last word in on a conversation that he was having with them. Not to mention turning their backs on him like he wasn't anything to them. But no matter how much he yelled at Earl to get his ass back here, he just waved him off. Tommy was so mad that he could feel his head pounding and his belly churn up. Leaning over to puke, he wasn't the least bit surprised to find that there was blood in his vomit.

It had been happening for the last week and a half that he'd get so upset that he'd throw up, and there would be blood in it. At first, it was only a little bit, but it was becoming worse the more his family stressed him out. This was all their fault, they were making him ill, and he wasn't going to allow them to feel badly for him. No, this was all their fault, and if he got sicker, he wasn't going to allow them near him.

"Dirty bastards, all of them." He left the plant after throwing up a couple more times. He hoped that someone would see it and tell on them. It had to be a code violation for them to have blood just lying around. Before he'd gone five feet from his mess, one of the workers had come out and hosed it off. He'd bet that they'd not tell his brother either that Tommy was puking up blood. "You'll all get yours in the end. See that you don't. All of you will pay for making me sick like this."

Making his way home, he tossed up about four more times. No one said anything to him about it, so he just puked where he happened to be standing. As soon as he was in his place, he got him some of the pink shit that he'd been taking all his life and drank half a bottle of it. Of course, it came right back up, looking pinker for the blood that was mixed in it now.

Going to bed, he let his head pound and was glad that Fred had stopped speaking to him for now. He didn't know if he could handle anything more today. He was just too sick to care what happened to the little voice or the man that would drive him crazy.

Chapter 6

Mandy watched her uncle as he laid on the bed with all kinds of tubes in him. He'd been found outside on his steps to his apartment covered in vomit and blood. It had taken them two days to figure out who he was, and by then, there had been a police report on him about him being missing. Not from anyone in the family, but the police were looking for him.

"What the hell are you doing in my house?" She got up and shook her mom awake when Tommy — she didn't like him enough to call him uncle anymore, but now that he was awake, her mom could deal with him. "I asked you a question. What are you doing in m — where the hell am I?"

"Hospital. You've been here for four days now." Her mom stood up and smiled at her. "Honey, if you want to go to the cafeteria now, I think that Edgar is coming, and he'll take you there."

"Thanks, Mom." She glared at Tommy. "You're not a nice person, are you? I thought you were, but you're just as mean as those boys that I go to school with. A mean person is all you are."

As soon as Edgar came into the room, she asked him to take her to get something to eat. After kissing Mom, he took her hand into his much larger one, and they made their way out again. It made her slightly sick to be around Tommy, and she didn't much care for hospitals either.

"What is it you wish to eat?" She couldn't help it, she burst into tears, and Edgar picked her up in his arms and found them a table way in the back of the room. "Oh honey, you're all right. He can't hurt you anymore. I promise you that I'll take care of him if he so much as looks at you funny."

"It's not just him. It's Levi, too." He asked her who that was. "When Mom and I were in Tennessee, this man moved into our house without Mom knowing about it. He would beat her up daily when she wouldn't just turn over her car keys to him and her money. Then he started on me, and we came up with this plan." She sat in the chair across from Edgar and didn't look at him while she finished. "Mom was so worried about me because he was getting worse all the time, but she couldn't get him out of the house. So...she really didn't want to do it, but I told her that it would be all right. And it was. She pushed me down the stairs."

"I'm sorry, what?" Mandy told Edgar that she had to do it to get her out of the unsafe house. "She pushed you down the stairs?"

"I had on this bike helmet and wrist braces on my arms. Even my legs were covered in this heavy moving material that we had when we moved into our house. She cried more than I did when the fall broke my leg. But once the ambulance got there, she was better. Not great, but better, and she went to the hospital with me. We never told anyone, but your brothers' wives figured it out and had Levi arrested for trespassing. As soon as he was in jail, Mom looked so much better. I don't want her brother to hurt me again, Edgar. If he does, I know that my mom will kill him, and she'll end up in prison."

He held her while she cried. It had been so long since anyone had held her like he was that she felt herself relaxing more and more. But when she sat up to finish her tale, he looked like he was upset. She asked him not to be mad at her mom.

"I'm not. I was just thinking how desperate she must have been to harm you. I'm very proud of her for thinking of things that would get you out of the house and away from that stranger. I'm going to talk to my sisters and ask them about it, too. The man needs to be dealt with, too."

"Don't go to prison. Please, just let him be." He said that he couldn't do that, but he'd not go to prison. "Sure you will. You're this great big dragon, and you'll kill him by chomping him up, and I don't want you to go to prison, either. He's out of our lives, and that's all that matters, right? Promise me that you'll let him go unless he comes around again."

"If he comes around again, I'm not going to hold back that much, I can promise you, love." He lifted up her chin with his finger and looked into her eyes. "You must be very proud of your mother for what she did with you. I am, as well. And I promise you that unless he comes around again, I will not kill him. Unless he does something to either of you again. Okay?"

"Yes, all right. I trust you, too." He kissed her on the cheek and asked her what she wanted to eat. "Just a piece of pie, if you don't mind. I've had the food here, and it's not all that great, is it?"

"No. And that's something that I have to talk to my dad about. The hospital is making things very difficult for the patients around here in not just the food but the meds as well." She watched him as he went to get her some pie, and when he came back, she was glad to see that he had a slice of his own. It wasn't like her mom's pie, but it was eatable. "You should taste my mom's apple pie. It's the best there ever was. She said that she puts some of her magic in it, but I don't know. We can't get enough of it when she does have time to bake."

"My mom loves to cook, too. She is good at it, too, but lately, we've been eating on the go. Just quick sandwiches that she can put together for the two of us to eat." Edgar said that he'd noticed that, too, that there wasn't as much time for meals of late. "When Grandpa and Grandma come in town, she'll have the cook make a big meal, but we're all so stressed out about Tommy that we don't eat all that much."

"He's going to be getting out of the hospital soon enough. Then he'll be back to his old tricks. You have to stay alert when you're out by yourself. He can still hurt you, and I'll kill him for that." She said that she was staying close to home now that she knew there was magic around it. "Good for you. I know that you know my parents well, so if you ever want to hang out with them, they'd love it. They'll take you to the other realm, too. You can see unicorns and dragons there."

"Mom told me that there are all kinds of magical creatures there that I'd not believe." He smiled and told her that there were gnomes, too, along with trolls as well. "I know. I would love to go there. Did you know that Mom's parents are my grandparents…Silly question, of course you do. Does that make your mom and dad my grandparents, too? I'd like to call them that. If you think it will be all right with them."

"You'd have to ask them, but I don't see them having a problem with it. You're their first grandchild. They love you already." She said she'd talk to them the next time she saw them. "I think they were hoping you'd come to the other realm and hang out with them for a few days while your grandparents are back home. They want to get to know you better."

"I'd love that too." She was so excited that she had to take three calming breaths before she felt she could talk again. "I've been hinting at calling your brothers and their wives aunt and uncle. I know they won't mind either, will they?"

"No, they'll love it too." She thought of all his brothers and thought that Edgar was the nicest of them all. She told him that. "Thank you for that, but Fowler is the smartest of all of us. He was born first and sort of tested the waters for us to go to college several times in our lifetime. My brothers and myself have been doctors and nurses, attorneys, as well as anything else you could think of. We've been around for a long time, so we've had plenty of time to study up on things that a normal person wouldn't be able to do. That's why I love doing contracts so much, I've had a great deal of practice at it."

"I bet you have." She looked at the doorway and saw her mom. "She looks upset again. I wonder what Tommy said to her that had her crying." She looked at him. "Don't kill him until you know for sure that she's crying over him, all right? I like having you around, and I won't be able to visit you very much if you're behind bars."

"I'll keep that in mind when I ask her what happened." She sat down with the two of them and leaned her head on Edgar's shoulder. Getting up, she wrapped her arm around her mom, too, and sat there for however long she'd let herself be pampered. Which turned out to be longer than she had expected. Sitting back in her chair, it was Edgar who asked her what had happened.

"He's pissed off because he's not in a private room with his own nurses. I don't have any idea why he thinks he should be getting that sort of treatment, but then he is Tommy." She looked over at her and smiled. "Did you want to go home tonight? I'm ready to fly back right now if it gets me away from his temper. Mom and Dad said they'd deal with him from now on."

"Did you at least get to tell him why he's in the hospital for?" She nodded and said that he thinks she poisoned him. "How do you poison someone that has an ulcer? He's just lucky someone found him before he bled to death. The moron. I don't like him all that much. I know you don't either."

"I don't. That's why I want to go home. Just to have my own things around me and back to work." When she said it like that, Mandy was glad to be going home, too. She wanted to be around her other uncles and hang out with the aunts. They were funny, and they'd been helping her with her magic, too. "We'll leave on the first flight out, even if it's midnight. I just want to be home."

It wasn't as simple as that, and she thought her mom knew it. They had to say goodbye to her grandparents and Uncle Earl. There were other things, too, like packing up. She was going to leave everything that she came with to have at her grandparent's house so that when she wanted, she could come back and be with them. Mandy was excited to be able to change her clothing like her mother could, and it saved her from not having a lot of things in her closet, too.

The first flight out was at eight the next morning. Which meant that they had to get up and be at the airport at five-thirty. She didn't care so long as she could go to bed when she got home and not have to wake up until she was rested. It had been a very long time since she'd been able to sleep late, and she was happy her mom said she could get up when she wanted. She knew she wouldn't sleep late, no later than eight in the morning, but it was nice to have the option of sleeping late if she could.

The flight didn't take all that long. It seemed like they were up in the air and down again in minutes. But she was happy to be home again, so it mattered little how long the flight took. She thought about Tommy when they were flying down the runway.

He'd been found covered in blood and vomit. It looked like he'd gotten so weak that he fell off the stairs and onto the pavement to his apartment. Once he was down, hitting his head hard enough to get stitches, he laid there for two days before anyone thought to check on him. Mandy was told that he didn't live in the best neighborhood. He was lucky no one had hurt him worse while he was lying in his own stuff.

After stitching him up, it took the police another day to figure out who he was. Someone had rolled him for his wallet and, having found nothing of use in it, had dumped it in the dumpster another block away. The hospital had no choice but to call them in when he was a John Doe to help with his identification. Mom had been called first, as she was the one who had been talking to the police about him before she'd left the area. Grandpa and Grandma had come into the hospital right away, and she and her mom had flown to the area the next afternoon.

"Was he mean to you, Mom?" She said that she didn't want to talk about it. That he was out of his head in pain. "I just bet he was. Probably taking it out on Grandda and Grandma now, too."

"More than likely. But they won't stay with him if he gets too mouthy. Dad had told him that he wasn't going to put up with his crap while he was there. That just made Tommy madder." She looked at her mom and could tell that she'd been hurt by his words again. "Let's just go home and have a nice meal and watch some television. That sounds like a good way to end this trip. Don't you two think so?"

Both she and Edgar agreed. She did wonder if her grandparents would make it back in two weeks after this thing with Tommy. They were going to help Mom get the house in order. Only a few of the bedrooms were fixed. And there was nothing in the dining room nor the kitchen area for them to eat in if they wanted. The living room had two old couches from their other home, but she hated them as much as Mom did. Levi had sat on them.

Her room wasn't too bad. She had her a desk now and her computer set up. The only thing that she didn't have was a bed. She'd been sleeping on an air mattress since they moved in. It wasn't that bad, but she wasn't sleeping well enough for it to continue. Mom said she could have any size bed that she wanted as the room was large enough to hold a king-sized mattress in it. She was going to take her up on that deal.

She knew that Edgar was sleeping down the hall from her mom. He'd been staying since after the grand opening. Mandy was glad that he was there. It did make her mom in a better mood when he could stay and then have a meal with them every day. But he had a job, too, and was just as busy as Mom was. School was supposed to start back up in a couple of days, and she was looking forward to making new friends. Something that she'd always been good at was making long-lasting friendships at school.

By the time she was off the plane and in the car to take them home, she was about as exhausted as she'd been in a while. Dozing on the way back to the house, she didn't pay much attention to what was being said around her until they mentioned Tommy again. How he'd left a message on Mom's phone, and it hadn't been all that nice.

"He's still wanting to kill us all. And the nerve of him thinking that I'd come back to Tennessee so that he could murder me when I get there." Mom was crying, and Edgar was just letting her rant. That's what she'd do when her mom was in that kind of mood. "We should have just let him die out there. That would have been easier on all of us. Stupid jackass. I dislike him more and more daily."

Going into the house, she went up to her bedroom. It was the place where she could think and be alone. She knew that being just a kid at seven, she couldn't do anything about Tommy, but she wished that she was older so that she could punch him in the face until he understood that he was being especially mean to her mom.

Climbing on her mattress, she was ready to take a nap when her own cell phone rang. Without seeing who it was, she turned it off and put it in her drawer. No one important knew her number, and she didn't feel like messing with someone who was just randomly dialing the number to pull a scam. Within minutes, she was sleeping, and that was fine by her.

~*~

Edgar needed some time with his dragon. He was pissed off enough as it was, and not allowing him to get out wasn't helping. The need to protect Mandy and Tabby was great, and his dragon wanted to snap some heads. Mostly Tommy's. He was in the other realm, the one where his parents lived twenty minutes after leaving the home that he shared with Tabby and her daughter.

"Are you all right?" His dad took a step back when he said that he wasn't. When he told him he was sorry for snapping, Dad asked him if Tabby was all right. "Yes, she and Mandy are fixing dinner, and I asked if I could have some time here. I needed to let my dragon go for a bit. That's what I'm here for."

"Then go, son. Do what you need to do while you're here. Your mom is with her mom right now, and they're in a meeting. I wish I could fly with you." He'd never said that before, and it startled him that his dad would wish something like that. "It's all right, son.

Go fly. I'll watch you. It's about as good."

Nodding once, he took a running leap and was shifted almost as soon as he was in the sky. His body was forming the dragon even as he saw his mom coming up from the ground as well. They flew together for another hour or so, and he did feel better. After landing in the beautiful grass and flowers, he felt better than he had in quite some time.

"You and I both needed that, I think." He thanked his mom for flying with him. "It was my pleasure. Your dad said you looked stressed out, and I thought that I'd find out why. But as soon as I was able to shift and hit the skies, I knew that I needed it as much as you did. It's been a stressful few months around here."

"At home, too. I want to badly to protect the two of them, but there is very little that I can do other than to be there when they get upset with him. Before I forget, Mandy wants to call you and Dad Grandda and Grandma. I hope you don't mind, but I told her that you'd love it. Will you?" She told him there was no greater gift than that he could have given her. "Well, act surprised when she asks you. She'd going to call the others aunt and uncle too."

"I shant tell your father. He'll be surprised better than I would be. I'd be shocked to know the truth. But to be someone's grandparents is wonderful. Thank you, son." She asked him how Tommy was doing. "His health is poor, we were told. He doesn't do drugs, not that they found any in his body, but he's not been eating well, and it's been making him sicker. The ulcer can be treated without an operation, but I don't think he'll do what is needed to get himself healthy again."

"No, and with his personality, he'll blame that on his family as well. The kid needs to see someone about his behavior. His human body can't take the stress of trying to be that much of a pain in the ass all the time. Something has to give." He agreed with his mom. "Also, while you're here, I wanted to go over the contract that you sent back from the mayor. I think you're right. We don't want to get involved in that stuff. It's too political."

"Good. I'll send it back in the morning." He stretched out, letting his body feel the grass beneath his feet, and smiled at his mom. "I need to get back. I'm sure she expected me an hour ago."

"I've spoken to her. She was worried about you, and I told her that we were flying together. She's fine with you spending time with me and your father." He thanked his mom. "No worries, son. Your dad is coming now. Someday soon, we're going to have to all get together and have dinner. I'd love that."

"So would I." After the three of them had a long talk, he made his way home. Mandy was still resting, and Tabby was making popcorn for their movie night. He hoped that Mandy would join them, but he didn't hold out much hope. She'd been tried on the plane, and he didn't think a couple of hours nap was going to get her very rested right now. He'd be surprised if she didn't sleep until late into tomorrow morning for all her exhaustion.

Watching the movie was more than his tired brain could handle, and he kept dozing off on the couch. By the time it was over, he, too, wanted to sleep late in the morning and made his way upstairs with Tabby. They didn't have the house to themselves, but it was quiet like they did. As soon as he left Tabby at her door, he staggered down to his own. He thought perhaps he was asleep before his head hit the pillow.

He woke up twice in the middle of the night. Once to go to the bathroom and the second time because he thought that he'd heard something in the hall. Getting up, making sure that he was quiet, he looked down the long hall and didn't see anything that looked like it was coming to get him. As he was headed back to his room, Fred appeared in his room.

"What's happened? Are you all right?" The little creature said he was fine and was embarrassed that he'd woken him. As he told him what had happened with Tommy after everyone left him tonight, he was laughing so hard that he had to hold his sides. "So he thought that he could manhandle a woman nurse, did he? I wish I could have seen her putting him in his place. That must have been hilarious."

"You don't know that half of it, sire. He then had to deal with the biggest nurse I've ever seen when he patted the younger one on the bottom. She nearly ripped his ear off when she turned him about to tell him to stop. I've never seen a human react so quickly." Fred was laughing, too, now. "The big man picked up Mr. Tommy and tossed him right into a chair and tied him there. He needs to be getting up more often, and he'd been complaining about it. So now that he's sitting in the chair, the big man sits right there with Mr. Tommy and flicks him with his fingers every time he gets out of control with his mouth. His toes will be sore tomorrow. You can bet your life on that."

"I bet so, too. Oh, you've no idea how much I needed to hear that, Fred. Thank you for sharing it with me." He said that he'd thought he and his missus could use a good laugh after today. "Yes, it's been a stressful day."

"Lord Edgar, there are two faeries that wish to work on the little one's room for her. She has expressed a desire to have her room done up with bunk beds and a dresser combination. I've never seen the likes that she wants, but they said that they have special magic that will allow them to help her with anything she wishes. I thought that I'd ask you before they approached her." He said that it would be up to her mother. That was something that he didn't have a clue about. "Yes, good idea. Asking the mother will sort things out quickly for her. Yes, you're very smart for telling me that. I will ask her in the morning before I head back. I have one of the other brownies watching over Mr. Tommy so that I could have a break from him. I hope that's all right."

"It's more than all right, Fred. You do what you need to do to get yourself whatever you need to keep an eye on him. When you were assigned this job, I never thought that it would be this long. And I'm sorry to have taken you away from your family. You should take a couple of days off so that you can rest too. I know that I needed it."

"I might do that, sir. My lady wife has been handling things for me since I've been gone. I'd like to have a couple of days to pamper her a bit for her helping me with this job. She's a good wife, and I love her very much." Edgar told him to enjoy his time at home and to stay as long as he needed. "No more than a couple of days, sire. I will need to go back and watch over him. I don't believe he's going to be doing well for some time now, and I'd better watch over him. It's a hard job, but I'm up for it."

"I couldn't have picked a better man for the job, I don't think." He embarrassed the little man and was glad that he was taking the job so seriously. He'd have to figure out a reward for him and his little family when this was all over. Edgar would ask his mom, and she'd know. Going back to bed when the little person left him, he fell asleep quicker this time and was out before he could make out the time on his phone.

Chapter 7

Making her way to his bedroom, she counted the chimes on the clock. It was six in the morning, the house was empty, and she wanted Edgar in the worst kind of way. She was sick of waiting for the right time.

It was totally her fault they'd never made love. He said he'd wait, and he had. She wondered if he had more stamina than she did or if she was just at her rope's end with him. Either way, today was the day, and she didn't want him to ask her if she was sure. Because no, she wasn't, but she was sure that she loved him with all her heart. Going into his bedroom, she was dismayed to find that he wasn't there. Frustrated now, she pulled her robe tighter around herself and went through the house one door at a time.

In the office, she heard a thud sound. It wasn't perfectly tuned like you'd hear in music, more of a chopping sound now that she thought about it. Looking out the window, she could see the lined-up wood between two big trees and Edgar out there shirtless, chopping wood with the biggest axe she'd ever seen. Now, she didn't know what to think.

Going back up to her room, she got dressed in something warmer and made her way down the stairs in time to see him coming into the house. She stood on the fifth step from the bottom, towering over him, and asked him what he'd been doing.

"Nothing. Just out for a bit." He was dressed now, and she thought that she'd missed something great when she'd not gotten to see him without his shirt very well. Damn it all to hell and back. Her timing couldn't have been worse. "What are you doing up so early?"

"I was looking for you." Down a step when he took one step toward her. "Are we going to have a particularly hard winter that you're aware of?" She took another step down when he took one toward her again. "You've been chopping wood like we're going to need that much."

"I've been chopping wood so that I don't go down the hall and sneak into your room and take you." Two more steps down to his two in front of her. "Mandy is gone. My mom picked her up earlier so that she could help with the faeries that will be born today. She's excited about it. Why are you dressed like that?"

"I was going to find you. I told you that." He nodded no more than a foot from her. "So the house is empty now, then, right? There is no one here but the two of us."

"Some staff in the kitchen, but I've sent them on their way. Did you know that our cook and her husband are members of the local wolf pack?" She nodded and told him that she'd known that. "Good. They'll be back tonight to cook dinner. That gives us hours before anyone will be returning."

"Did you have some plans for the empty house today?" He nodded no more than inches between the two of them. "You have dust in your hair. It must have been wood shavings. Are you going to just stand here, or did you want something from me?"

"Yes. Everything." He pulled her into his arms and kissed her while her feet never touched the floor. When they entered the office where he'd been working, she was both disappointed and excited at the same time, thinking that he was going to take her on the floor. But all he did was turn her toward the door and lift her up to where her breasts were at his mouth. He soaked her blouse while biting through the material.

Her nipples hardened, and he slid her down the wall, bracing her against it by putting his knee between her legs and holding her up. Taking her blouse into his hands at either side, he ripped it open by tearing each of the buttons off it, scattering them to the floor.

Her bra fared no better as it was torn from her body by one of his very sharp nails that had to have come from his dragon. Christ, she could feel her pussy weep with need just then, and it embarrassed her slightly.

"I want you. Now." Yes, she answered him, now would be good. "I'm sorry this is going to be so quick. The next time, I promise to be gentle."

Ripping her pants off with her panties, her breath caught in her throat. He was going to take her right here against the wall, and she couldn't wait for him to do it. As soon as he tore at his own clothing, making a shredded mess of them, he slammed his cock into her without any thought that she could take him.

He filled her to the back of her throat. Every part of her body felt like it had been taken by his cock. Her nipples hardened painfully more, and her fingers tingled with excitement. And it felt wonderful. As soon as he started to move, quick hard punches to her pussy, she held onto his shoulders, knowing that when he came, he was going to fill her body.

His mouth moved along her chin. As soon as he got to her throat, Tabby was sure that he could feel her pulse and when he bit down, hard and painfully, she screamed out her release as it caught her unawares.

She saw unicorns and trolls. Dragons and queens. Stars danced around her vision as she held onto Edgar like her life depended on it. As her body rose up, seemingly to the stars, she leaned into his throat and bit him, too.

The heat of his blood filled her mouth. It wasn't coppery like she thought it would be but sweet like manna. When he shouted out that he was coming, her body braced itself for his cum, and when he filled her up, her body sored above the stars and beyond. Then there was nothing.

She must have only been out for seconds. Edgar was telling her how sorry he was and that he loved her. Lifting her head from his wounded shoulder, she licked his wound closed and looked at him. The buzzing in her head was getting louder, and she cried out when it took her under again.

Waking up, she was in Edgar's arms, and he was sitting on the floor. She didn't know how she'd gotten there, and with his head tilted back and his eyes closed, she didn't want to bother him with questions right now. He looked up at her suddenly, and she had a smile. She didn't know how he'd gotten it, but he had a black eye that she'd not noticed before.

"You're very violent when you come, aren't you?" She said that she didn't know as that was the first time she thought she'd ever had a climax before. "Really? Even with Mandy's father?"

"He was a one-time thing, and I was too young to appreciate anything when it was going on. I was sixteen when I had her, and I've not dated too much since then. Men don't seem to care for a woman who has a child that is as tall as she is."

"Those men have no idea what they're missing out on." She agreed with him and started to rise up. "Are we finished here?"

"We're not?" He shook his head and winked at her. "You're very charming when you want to be, aren't you?" He told her that he could smell her instant arousal. His cock hardened incredibly harder as he sat there on the floor.

"Lean into the chair. Put your hands on the back of it for me."

When she moved forward to do as he asked and, she realized what he was going to do, and her body wept for him.

"That's it, baby. Now spread your legs wide for me. I'm going to fuck you like this. Take you from behind and make you come. Are you sore? I can...I will try not to be so rough, but I need to be deep inside of you."

"We have a mess to clean up here. There are buttons all over the room from my blouse." She bent over to pick up a button when she heard him moan. "We're going to be late all day if you keep this up."

She moaned when he leaned in to nip at her ass cheek, just breaking the skin and then licking the tiny wound closed. Being this close to her heat, it was all she could do not to drop to her knees and taste him. Suckle from his cock until she had her fill of him. Standing, he bent his knees slightly and slowly entered her from behind, moving into her wet hot pussy and stopping. His body was so close to spilling inside of her that she needed a moment to gather herself.

"Edgar, if you don't move inside of me, I'm going to hurt you. You know I can, too."

Her voice was husky with her need. Heat from her surrounded his cock, and his balls tightened up closer to his body. He put his hands on her hips and moved deeper within her.

When he was seated fully inside of her, he began to slide in and out, gripping her hips hard. There would be a mark, a deep bruise, but she did not care. He seemed to be mesmerized by the slickness of his cock as it moved in and out of her, wet with her cream and hard for her body. Her need to mark him, to fill her with his seed paramount to anything else at the moment, and she moaned at the thought of him shooting his cum deep into her womb again. He shifted to his left slightly and watched her breast jerk with each slam of his cock into her.

"Oh, Christ, Tabby, you're so tight. Every time you bent over to pick something up, it was all I could do not to come all over myself. But this is so much better. Slamming deep in you. I love being buried deep in this pussy. Soon, love, I'm going to fuck this sweet ass of yours. I'm going to fuck you here until you scream."

He stuck his thumb in his mouth to wet it and pressed it hard against her tiny rose. When her body jerked tight against his, he nearly lost his control. His movements became frantic as his need to come and bring her with him moved over them both.

"Please, Edgar. Harder. Fuck me harder. I'm so close, so very close. I want to feel your cum inside me. Now, please, now!"

He started slamming into her hard and fast. Each time he slammed deep, she would feel her sheath pull him in tighter and squeeze around him. When she stood up, pulling him with her, she leaned into his chest, bringing her hands up to his neck. He cupped her breast and pulled hard on her taunt nipples. She suddenly needed more and pulled from him. He jerked her around to face him and picked her up by her ass and slammed her against the wall, and entered her again just as she wrapped her legs tightly around his hips. Tabby wrapped her hand to the back of his head, grabbed a handful of his hair, and yanked his head back, exposing his throat.

"Bite me! Fuck Tabby, bite me hard!"

She sank her teeth hard into his throat, right where the pulse was pounding as hard as he was into her. She broke his skin and marked him with her bite, bruising the tender flesh. She felt his blood fill her mouth. He jerked his head forward, pulling his own hair, and bit her at the closest place he could sink his teeth. Their release roared through them, their mutual climax nearly violent in its release.

Breathless, they stood where they were and didn't move. The two of them had had sex twice, and neither time did it happen in their bed. From now on she was going to go looking for him in her nudity and see what other tricks he had up his...naked arm.

"Are you sore? Because I know that I'm going to be." She asked him about all the wood he chopped. "Not the same muscles were used, thankfully. I might have died a thousand deaths had I been using the same muscles and tried to fuck you too."

"I suppose." She was getting a cramp in her foot but was too relaxed to move right then. Something else occurred to her. "I'm starving. You must be, too. How about we move — as much as I hate to do that, clean up our mess in here, and have some breakfast?"

"I'm up for that." It took them twenty minutes to find the last button. And Edgar found it caught in one of the curtains nearest the desk. That would have been way more embarrassing than finding it on the floor, she thought. But she was safe from embarrassment because she wouldn't allow him to quit looking until they found them all.

Breakfast was after they took a shower and got

cleaned up. She wanted to go back to bed and take a nap, but they both had things to get finished up. Tabby had an interview to complete for the person who was going to be working on her days off—something that she was going to do was to take one or two days a week off so she didn't have burnout. And she was going to spend those days with her new husband and her daughter.

Going into the kitchen to cook, she felt an eerie kind of something roll over her. Looking around, she didn't see anything out of the ordinary, so she went back to work making pancakes for the two of them. Edgar came into the kitchen with his cell phone to his ear, and he looked like there was something bad going on.

"Tommy was spotted not three miles from here." Nodding, she was suddenly not hungry and wanted to find her daughter. "One of the merchants in town talked to him, and he was looking for you. He said that he looked a little worse for wear but knew it was him."

When he got off the phone, she asked about Mandy. He told her that she couldn't be in a safer place than with his mom and grandma. That didn't thrill her, but she knew he was right, that she'd be better off with them than she would be with her here.

"No one is giving him any information. He'll not

be able to come into the house or the yard. Remember that. The merchant didn't know if he had a gun or not, but he said that Tommy was saying that he was looking for you because you owed him some money." She was trying hard to keep her emotions at bay. This was no time to panic. When Edgar reached for her hand, she took it like a lifeline and held it to her heart. "He's not going to be able to get to you so long as you stay inside the house. If you need to go to the plant, I can have my mom take you there with her magic. But I'd rather you stayed here until we figure out what he wants."

"Money." She looked at him. "My parents. Are they all right? How did he get here without any money? Oh, Edgar, I'm terrified for my family."

"He stole a plane ticket. My dad is tracking him now. He's the best there is at tracking someone." She nodded, afraid more than she'd ever been in her life. "He won't kill him because he's the humans' problem, but he will keep tracking him and let us know where he is at a moment's notice."

"Can he get into the plant even though I'm not there? That could be drastic for a lot of people. I don't want anyone hurt." Edgar told her that he couldn't harm the place. "Good. I hate this. I just want him to realize that he's not getting anything from me and for him to go on with his life. But he'll never do that since he believes that we owe him somehow."

"No. He can't harm the building in Tennessee, either. Things are going well for—Dad found him, and he's at the end of our driveway. He said that he's shouting out your name to get you to come and take the magic away from the gate." She went to the front of the house and looked out the window. She could see him now and told Edgar. "He killed the man that he took the ticket from. They only just found his body and are looking for his killer. Dad said to assume that he has a gun as that's how he killed Mr. Trenor at the airport."

"I'm going to call my parents. All right?" Edgar said that he'd deal with Tommy while she was on the phone. "Don't go out there, Edgar. You said that he could hurt you."

"I'm going to shift into my dragon and scare him a bit." She wanted to see him doing that but needed to hear from her mom and dad right now. After getting her dad on the phone, she burst into tears while telling him what was going on. Mom assured her, too, that she was all right. "I have to get in touch with Earl too. I need to hear that he's all right as well."

"He's here. We were having lunch together, so he's fine too." Relief like she'd never felt washed over her, and she couldn't believe how much better she felt.

"Honey, just stay in the house and let Edgar handle things. I wish I could see his dragon. I sure do.

But that'll have to be at another time."

She watched as Edgar shifted, and his giant dragon filled the space from the house to the end of the road. He was magnificent in the sunlight, and she couldn't believe how lucky she was that he was all hers. She told her dad that Tommy had run away as soon as Edgar shifted at him.

"Good man, that husband of yours. Goodness, it's good to know that he can do that and keep my baby girl safe." She agreed with her dad on that. "Now that you know we're safe, you go on now and help Edgar. He might not know it yet, but he needs you by his side when dealing with your brother. You know him better than anyone else." She told him that she'd be right there for him whenever he needed her.

She didn't venture outside, but she was happy to watch as Edgar laid in the yard, ready for anything. When Edgar turned and shifted again, she opened the door to let him in. That was when she saw her brother again.

~*~

Tommy fired the gun three more times when his sister didn't so much as fall over from his shots. He knew that he'd hit her, all five times he'd shot at her, but there she was—he was so focused on Tabby that he'd forgotten all about the giant dragon that had been lying in the yard. But he was more afraid of the man that was walking toward him.

"You can't kill her." He fired once more at the man, Eddy, something. "It's Edgar, not Eddy. And you can't kill me either. Your bullets are worthless coming onto our land like this. You can't kill either of us, and that makes me very happy."

"She owes me fucking money. I want her dead." Edgar told him that wasn't going to happen. He might as well give it up. "No. I'm going to kill her and that brat. Then I'm going to kill you too. And anyone else that gets in my way."

"You can try, but it's not going to get you anywhere." He heard the sirens just as Edgar pointed them out to him. "You're going to be arrested for trying to kill us, and that will put you in jail long enough for you to be examined by some very good doctors. Your family thinks that there is something wrong with you to have you acting out like this. I think you're just a greedy — go ahead, fire all you want at me. The police are watching you now."

Tommy kept firing long after he knew that the gun was emptied. Finally, when none of his planning was going right, he threw the weapon at Edgar, and had he not moved, it would have hit him in the head. Nothing was going right for him today or even the last few weeks, and he was going to have his head explode if he didn't get something for it soon. He leaned over and threw up more blood than he'd seen in a long time.

Seeing the blood made him sicker still, and he threw up twice more before he was tackled from behind and rolled to the grassy front lawn of his sister's place.

"I'm dying." The officer that had thrown him to the ground didn't say anything to him. The one standing beside the two of them, his gun out and pointed at him, read him his rights. Like he didn't already know them by heart. "You have to help me. I'm dying. I'm bleeding to death as I sit here."

"You'll be going to jail, buddy. Then, to the hospital. An ambulance is on its way to determine if you need medical help right away. Until then, you'll be cuffed and held right where you're sitting."

When the ambulance finally showed up, he'd tossed his stomach up four more times. He was getting weak from all the blood loss, and he didn't know how much longer he could remain sitting upright. The officer with the gun said he was going to shoot him if he didn't sit still. He decided to bargain with them to see if he could get some money from his sister.

"I don't know what's going on, but I was supposed to meet my sister here, and she was going to give me some money. Her husband, he's not too keen on her handing over some cash to me, and we had a little disagreement." He thought about that for a second. "He hits her, you see. Knocks her around a bunch and doesn't like me to interfere in their lives. But she owes me some money from the last time that she got knocked around."

"You're saying that Edgar Walsh knocked around his pretty new wife? I don't believe that's even possible. Did you hear that, guys? He said that Edgar is a wife abuser." They all thought that was like some kind of joke, and they were laughing about it. "Edgar's mother would knock him three ways from Sunday if he even thought about touching his wife with harm. Then, his daddy would take over if there was anything left of him. Nah, you should have come up with a better lie, Tommy Boy. That one doesn't hold water." He laughed again. "Edgar hitting his wife. That's just too funny."

"Well, he did." They were all laughing at him, and he was ready to get up and knock the shit out of them all. But the medics were saying that he needed to go to the hospital and he'd need an escort there by one of the officers. "Just get my sister out here right now and make her turn some money over to me. It won't take but a minute. She'll hand it over with you guys around. She knows she owes it to me. They took my name off the letterhead and made it so that I can't get into the bank and take what I want. I can't even get into the plant anymore."

"Sounds to me like someone is watching their

backs with you around. Also, sounds like they know you better than we do, and they're not going to be turning over anything to you in the near future." The cop with the gun finally put it in his holster. There wasn't any place for him to go as he had two IVs in his arms, and they'd given him something for pain. Tommy felt good for a few minutes until he saw Edgar and Tabby standing over him. "Are you pressing charges, Mr. Walsh? Mrs. Walsh? We saw him firing a gun in your direction. Are either of you hurt?"

"Yes, we wish to press charges. And no, neither of us was hurt by his gun. I'm just glad that he's a terrible shot, or we might well have been killed by him coming around here." Tabby said that she was glad that her daughter wasn't around, or she might well have been hurt by her brother.

"I'm going to kill her, too, and her little dog. You'd better be watching your stairs, little sister. I'm gunning with my gun for you." He laughed, thinking of the joke he'd just told about gunning her down with a gun. He'd never felt so odd before. "Hey, what did you give me? That has me thinking I'm funny."

"So you were planning on killing your sister and her daughter, were you? That's against the law, you understand." He told the officer that what he understood was that he had to kill her to be able to pay for the insurance policies.

"They make you have to wait four months… or ninety days? How many months is that?" Someone told him. "Yes, three months. You have to wait three months before you can cash in the one million dollar policy that I've taken out on the rest of the family. My momma is going to not like me much, but she's gotta go too. All of them do so I can have some flashing around money."

"You're going to kill your entire family? Then what are you going to do when they're all gone?" He said he'd been putting some thought into that and figured that he'd just have to figure out some random people's names and kill them off, too. "Sounds like you've got this all worked out, young man. I'm sure that the police sergeant will be thrilled to hear you confessing everything."

"You betcha." He looked up at Eddy again. "No, it's Edgar. He's my brother-in-law, Edgar. He changed into a big dragon. You should have been here earlier. He was this monster of a dragon just lying in the yard. I was sure that he was going to eat me. Weren't you, Edgar Washburn?"

"Sure I was, Tommy. Sure I was. And I'd not eat you. I'd be worried about getting sick on the poisons that are you." Tommy thought that was funny and was dismayed that no one laughed. "You're acting like you're drunk. Did you know that?"

"I have a reaction to drugs that way." He hiccuped. "That's why I don't take them no more. They affect me like I'm on a bender blender. Get it? Bender blender? 'Cause you need a blender to make drinks. Get it?"

He knew that he was funny, but none of the people around him was laughing. His dad told him once that when he was getting teeth pulled, he had said he was going to fuck the pig in the yard. Then he thought of his dad.

"Where is my daddy and mommy? They should be here too with Earl. That way, I can get you all in one place and kill you off. Off with your heads. See? I'm funny. But if you could get them all here, and I can just borrow one of your guns, I could just tick off my list the people that I'm going to kill. I need some money."

"You're not going to be killing anyone, Tommy. You're going to jail." He told Tabby to shut her lying mouth. "I'm happy that you're going to jail, and I hope you're there for a very long time, too."

"You liar. That's all you've ever done is lie to me. And about me. Why did you tell Dad and Earl how to keep me out of the safe? That wasn't very sisterlike of you, Tabby. You should be nicer to me. I could kill you right now, and that would be the end of you. But I tell you what. You give me some money, a lot of money, and I'll kill that brat of yours right quick. Just one bullet to the head, and that will be it for her and you."

Suddenly, he was moving, and he couldn't use his arms or legs. They had him tied up to the bed he was on and taking him someplace. Yelling at Tabby to tell them to let him go, all he got from her was her back turned to him. Christ, he hated that more than he did anything in the world. He wasn't finished with her yet, and she was walking away. Or was he moving? He couldn't tell right then.

"I'm back. Well, now you've done it. You've gotten yourself arrested." It was Fred again. He asked him where he'd been. "Hiding from you. So you know, no one but you can hear me. I think I like that better, don't you? But the others. They were afraid that you'd harm me, so I was staying with my lady wife for a few days. I can tell that I missed a great deal. You're off to jail, I see."

"Nope, they're taking me to hospital first. I've been puking up blood. They don't know it yet, but I think maybe I've been dying for a while now, and no one noticed. But as soon as I get me some money, I'll be right as raindrops." The man next to him, he thought he was one of the medics, asked him who he was talking to. "Fred. He's not a friend of mine, but he does know a great deal about me. Reads my mind, you see. Tells on me, too, when he thinks I'm being bad. I'm always bad, don't you agree?"

"Yes, you're going to let people think you're insane if you keep talking like you are. People can't hear me, Tommy boy. I told you all you have to do is think about what you're saying, and I'll hear you. Right now, well, boyo, you're going to be going to the funny farm if you keep this up."

Chapter 8

Melbourne kept a running tale about Tommy to his brother. Then Edgar was relaying it to Tabby. Tabby was really stressed out, and he didn't blame her. Her own brother had tried to kill her and her little girl. They were the nicest people in the world, and he'd been stressing all day about him, too.

"They're taking him to surgery to try and stop the bleeding. They're also looking into the blood bank to get him a transfusion or something. I've never been a doctor, so I'm not sure what the protocol is about it." Edgar told him it had been too long for him, and he wasn't sure anymore, either. "He keeps talking to Fred out loud. It's funny. Fred keeps telling him that he's mind speaking with him, but either he doesn't get it, or he just doesn't care. Either way, they're thinking that he's lost a couple of marbles along with a lot of blood."

"Mr. Walsh, you asked to be notified if there was anything that you could do for Mr. Reader? Do you know your blood type?" He told him as much as he wanted to, he couldn't donate any blood. "Well, if you know of anyone that could, I'm sure that it would go a long way in helping with his recovery."

He told his brother what was going on. "Tabby can't donate either. Can you imagine what they'd say when they try and get a blood type from her? It would be funny if not so dangerous to us, too."

Melbourne went to the waiting room but kept a tab on the doctor doing the surgery. He told his brother that things were going well in the surgery, and they were just going to make sure to stop the bleeding. Once they had that done, then they'd take care of the ulcer that was eating away at his stomach.

"They're thinking that there is so much damage done that they might have to take out a lot more of his stomach than they thought. If so, then he'll have to have a colostomy bag for the rest of his life." Edgar said he'd not like that. "I don't know that anyone would like that big brother."

"Yes, you're right. Tabby said that it would be worse on him, being that his image is everything to him. Thanks for being there with him, Melbourne. The press has been camped out at our house since he was arrested wanting a scoop or something."

"I'm just glad I was around here so I could go by. I mean, you could have done what I'm doing from where you are, but this makes it seem like you're getting information from a nurse and not through our mind links." He laughed a little. "Fred is with me now.

He looks more rested than he did when I saw him the other day. I hope that his few days off were a good time for him and his family."

"I didn't know he had a family, to be honest. But I also found out that the faerie with Earl has a family as well. We'll have to keep an eye on those little people to make sure that they're getting family life as well." Melbourne told him that he was sending Fred home as there was nothing he could do for Tommy now that he was in surgery. "Good idea. Yeah, that's great. Tell him thanks for us, too. He's done a good job of keeping us informed about what he was up to. I don't know what we would have done had we not known about his bleeding sooner rather than later. They said that Tommy had lost a great deal of blood.

Melbourne kept a running update on Tommy and his surgery. Once it was determined that he'd not need to have a colostomy bag for him to live, they decided that he was going to have to follow a diet that would help him retain his weight at a good level as well as keep him alive. Any more surgeries to his belly would be dangerous. Melbourne thought that Tommy would abuse his health as he had done all along, and he'd be dead within a couple of years because of it.

Mr. Walsh, there's a phone call for you. It's at the nurse's station." He thanked the young woman and made his way there. He didn't know who it would be as he had a cell phone, and his family would have reached out to him through their link. Saying his name, he was no closer to figuring out who it was than he'd been before.

"You probably don't remember me, but my name is Clara Winter. We went to college together back in the fifties." He told her he was sorry, but he'd not gone to college in the fifties, but maybe she had mistaken him for one of his brothers. "No, I'm sure that it's you. We had chemistry together with Mrs. Banton. Please say that you remember me."

"I'm sorry, but I don't. What can I do for you?" She told him nothing much, but she wanted him to find her granddaughter for her. "I don't know what you think it is that I can do for you, Ms. Winter, but I don't find missing people. I work with my family in businesses across the country."

Reaching out to his family, he asked them if they might know who she was. It was Sidney who got back to him and then reminded him that they had helped when one of the students had gone missing, and they'd found her body not far from campus. Ms. Winter was talking about the girl's body when he tuned into her conversation with him.

"Ms. Winter, my brother reminded me that it was another student who had gone missing at the campus in the state we live in, but none of them were students at the time." She said she must have been mistaken and told him she was sorry. "Don't be. I can try and help you find her. How long has she been missing."

"Five years. I know that it's a long time to hold out hope that she's still alive, but I don't believe that she's gone. No one will help me find her when I've been raising her little boy since the last time I saw her." He asked her if she had any proof that she was still alive. "She keeps using my credit card that I gave her that day to buy her son some milk and baby food. It's never a lot, and I wouldn't even realize it, but there is a charge on there for some gasoline, and I don't own a car. Nor do I know how to drive." He asked her when that was. "Last month. I only get my statements once a month or so, and I noticed it after the first time that it had been used. I think that she's out there and afraid to come home."

"What would be her reason for not coming home?" The nurses were listening intently, and he decided to get Ms. Winter to call him on his cell phone. Then, he wouldn't be tying up their lines at the desk. After making sure that she had the right number, he cut off the call and went back to his seat in the waiting room. "I asked what reason she'd be afraid to come home."

"Her husband. He's not filed for divorce because

he said that he doesn't believe in it. He doesn't have a thing to do with Caleb, but he does come around asking me if I've heard from her. I never tell him that I do and that I think she's hiding out from him." He asked if it was an abusive relationship. "Yes, very bad one. He beat her nearly to death on their honeymoon when he realized that she wasn't a virgin. She swore to him that she was that she'd never had sex before him, but he wanted her to be hurting after sex—I'm sorry, I don't know why I'm telling you all this. I could have just said that he beat her a great deal."

"That's all right, Ms. Winter." She asked him to call her Clara as she thought that they might be around the same age. "I'm busy at the moment, but I'll come and see you as soon as I'm able. Give me your address and phone number, and when I have some time, I'll come and see you at your house. Will that be all right?"

"Perfect. Daniel is in jail right now, so he'll not know that I'm seeking help. I had hopes that Rachel would come to see me while he was away, but so far, nothing. The police told me that if she wanted to be found, she would be. They think that she's dead and that I'm a crazy old woman who doesn't have anything else to do but to call them up on occasion. I've given up on them finding her for any reason." After he got her address and phone number, he asked her to keep track of when she used the card, and that might lead them to find her. "I told the police that, but they said I could have done it on my own. I don't have a stupid car, I told the idiots. That was six months ago, and I've been keeping track since then. She's used it for other things too. I get a running description from my card company on what it's been used for."

She didn't live that far from the hospital and figured that he'd go there and find out what he could do. Perhaps he'd find that it was all just a scam to get him to come to her house, but he wasn't worried. He was a large dragon, after all. Closing the call, he told his brothers where he was headed in the event he might need them and left the hospital.

The house was a neat little row house with a nice front yard that needed a bit of mowing and some weeding. It was not too bad, but it looked like it had needed it for a few days. There were flowers planted along the sidewalk, with more flowers in hanging baskets hanging from the porch roof. The color of the house, not at all like the white of her neighbors, was bright blue and stood out like it was supposed to. He'd bet anything that she'd have no difficulties getting things delivered to her if she just said what color her house was. There wasn't another one on the street with any color at all. He knocked on the door and was greeted by a young boy of about six, and his smile was as bright as the house and flowers around them.

"I'm to meet your grandmother. She called to ask me to help her." He backed up and allowed him entrance, but he couldn't enter without the grandmother allowing him to. He was part vampire, and that was one of the things that he got from his dad.

"You're a vampire." She'd not asked, but he told her that he was part of one, and the other half of him was a shifter. "I didn't know that. Are we gonna be safe with you around?"

"As safe as I can make you, my lady." She nodded and invited him in, and he felt the warmth of the house and the love there immediately. "This house is full of love and good vibes. There is a little bit of violence by the door, but nothing much that I can tell."

"That'll be because of Daniel. He likes to come over and make his point by beating on my door and yelling things at us. We don't much care for it, but I don't let him in either. My daughter was part wolf from her daddy's side of the family. My daughter and him passed away a few years ago, about ten, I guess now, and I've been keeping an eye on the family since." She eyed him. "You're not nearly as old-looking as I thought you'd be either. Must be the vampire in you."

"Some of it, yes." He was invited to have some tea and cookies with young Caleb. "I'd enjoy that a great deal."

After tossing the little boy's hair around, he

not only knew where the daughter was but that she was indeed hiding from her husband. She, even after all these years, carried some of the wounds that he'd given her just before she'd run away. This was a little more of the magic that he got from his parents in that he could touch an object that was well-loved by someone and find them without any trouble. But his debate now was to figure out how much he should tell the woman about the girl.

He decided to read her mind to figure out what kind of scam this might be or if she was telling the truth about trying to find her. He found her mind to be clear of anything but the idea of finding her granddaughter because she was dying and couldn't take care of the little boy much longer. It was sad, really. She'd given most of her life to taking care of her family, and when she's needed the most, she couldn't do it. All Clara wanted was for her babies to be safe, and they wouldn't be with Daniel around.

"I have this ability that I don't tell many people about and that I can find people when they're missing. I know not only is she alive but where she is too. You're right, she's not far away." Clara sat down hard in the chair across from him. "Don't faint on me. I know that she's at the neighbor's and has been all this time. She figured that Daniel would think she'd left for good at some long-distance place. She was using the card so you'd know that she was still alive and well."

"My poor baby. I don't know what to do about this sort of information. Should I contact her or just let her be?" He said he didn't know, but she was all right and missing the two of them a great deal. "I guess she might well have been keeping tabs on us...Mr. Grander, that's who she's staying with, always takes pictures of my grandson. He said that he takes them to show his wife at the cemetery. I never thought a thing about it. What a good friend he's been, and I didn't know it."

After a little bit, he reached out to Mr. Grander, finding out that he was a wolf, too. He didn't know if the connection would be one he could get, but he did try. He couldn't believe it when he not only spoke to the older man, but he was coming over with Rachel right then. With Daniel in jail right now, they could have a nice visit without him ever knowing. Taking full advantage of his vampire blood, he made it so there were shadows all around the young woman when she got out of the car and into the house.

"I don't know if he has the neighbors in his pocket, and I figured this was the safest way to get her in and out." That got him a hug from both women. "Thank you so much. I'm going to go to the police station and try to figure out how long Daniel is going to be in jail for and see what he's done to get himself there."

He left, and the neighbor on the left was out on her porch watering her plants, but she seemed to be keeping a keen eye on the house, too. When he said hello to her, she asked him what he was doing at the house, and he told her that he and Clara had been friends a long time ago.

"She ain't got no friends. Nobody visits her either." He said that she was wrong and he was proof that they were indeed friends. "No, you're sneaking around that woman. Helping her find her long-lost granddaughter. I see how you are. You should be helping that husband of hers find her. She's got a kid to raise with him, and they're not together."

"You seem to know a lot about her and her granddaughter. Did it ever occur to you that you could have been helping her around the house some? That she could have used your help with that little boy? Perhaps she's finally asking for help from Mr. Grander with her yard. It sure could use a good mowing around it." She huffed at him and went into her house. But that didn't stop her from sneaking peeks out of her curtain. "Old bitty."

Making his way to the jail, he did reach out to Mr. Grander and told him about the neighbor. He said he'd go out and mow the lawn now so she'd not have anything to report. Didn't cost him a dime, he told him to mow and to do a little weeding. And he was thinking about getting with the pack to have them do some things around the house, too.

Melbourne thought when he got back to the house that there would be others around making repairs to the front porch swing as well, and the weeds would be gone from her pretty posies.

Daniel was in jail for knocking over a mailbox. A serious crime in and of itself, but he had also peed on the mail that had been scattered around when he'd knocked it down. Those were serious crimes, and they were waiting for the judge to come through town and have his sentencing. Melbourne reached for his dad and told him what was going on. Dad, he knew, had friends in high places, and it might just work out for the little town and Clara, too.

"I'll take care of that for you. Clara Winter was a good friend to your aunt Rain, too. I'll have to tell her what's going on and see if she wants to get in on taking care of her." Dad laughed after a few minutes or so. "His court date is for next week, and that neighbor has been bringing him in dinners since he's been arrested. She's his mother. Rain is going to come to town and see to her needing help. She hadn't realized that her home needed some repairs either."

He told him how the pack was going to be taking care of it since the daughter and the little boy were part wolves. Dad told him that they should have been taking care of her all along since she was raising that little boy, but he didn't go into much with that. Melbourne was sore as he was standing there that his dad would pull enough strings that Clara would have meals brought to her and little Caleb as well as help with her bills. Wolves were a good lot, and they helped their own. He could only think that they didn't know what was going on with Clara and her great-grandson, or they would have been doing it all along.

He didn't know what he expected when he saw Daniel Crow. He envisioned a tall man with muscles from working out and a nice trimmed haircut. He couldn't have been more the opposite. Daniel was short, fat, and his hair was in dreadlocks that looked as if they'd grown out a great deal, like past his big butt, and he wasn't taking care of them. In all, he was a mess, and there was an odor about him that made Melbourne sort of sick to his belly. Like he'd not bathed in the weeks since he'd been in jail. He asked one of the officers about him.

"Won't bathe at all. We've threatened to bring in a hose to hose him down, but since the Captain won't allow us to do that, something about it being against his rights or some horse poop, we can't even go back to take him his trays without feeling like we're going to toss our cookies. Man, but he smells." He asked about what he was in for. "Damage to federal property, not to mention the mail that was in it. He's going to prison for that. There will be fines, too, that he'll have on top of jail time. Hopefully, it's not around here. I don't know if I could take a few more months of the way he smells or not."

"Did you ever have an occasion to look into the disappearance of Rachel Crow? Her grandmother asked me to help her look for her." He said that he'd not, but then he'd only been in the station for the last few weeks. He'd been transferred into the station house from another state. "She's been missing for about five years. I think her grandmother said she comes in here a few days a month."

"You mean crazy, Clara? Yes, I've heard about her. The boys tried to tell her that she was gone, that Daniel must have killed her. Then he buried her in some shallow grave someplace. Without a body, we got no case against him." Melbourne said that wasn't true, not in the state of Ohio. They didn't need a body to have him arrested. "I didn't know that. I'm going to have to look into that, of course, now."

Melbourne had a feeling that no one would go looking for poor Rachel and her supposed grave now, either. If this was the way the police had been running things around here, it was a small wonder that anything ever got done. He wondered how many other murders had been committed, and they sat on their collective asses. He left the station house before he cleaned house with his dragon.

As tempting as it would be, it would be a lot of paperwork as well. Laughing to himself, he decided that next term, he might run for mayor of this city just to clear out the cops. He found himself telling his dad what was going on.

"You're joking." He told him he only wished that he had been. "I'm going to make some calls around to some friends of mine. The thing is, they could have found her at any time had they just looked around in their own town. I don't know what makes me madder. Them calling Clara a crazy old woman or the fact that they don't know the laws in their own community. Not to mention state rules that they're supposed to be enforcing."

His dad used to be a cop and had been on a domestic call where he was supposed to be killed when he was taken away by magic. The queen of the earth, Melbourne's grandmother at the time, had saved him because he was mated to her granddaughter, Melbourne's mom.

He had no doubt that by the end of the day, heads would be rolling. His dad wouldn't be the one to do it, but the Federal Bureau of Investigation would certainly have a few things to say about it.

~*~

"Sammy, there's a phone call for you. It's your sister." She didn't go into panic mode like she normally did when there was a call for her but made her way to the community phone, just taking her time. "She said to remind you that it's her birthday and that you should be wanting to do something nice for her."

"Nice? I don't suppose she gave you a price range as to what this nice gift is going to cost me, did she?" The cook told her no, she'd not, but like always, it was going to cost a great deal. "You got that right. I'll tell you what it is if you want to formulate a price range while I'm talking to her."

"You gonna tell her no, aren't you?" She just stared at him. "Yeah, I hope so. She sounds really excited, so I'm going to assume that it's a really nice gift you got for her."

"She works, so I don't understand why... it doesn't matter. I'm not going to pay for anything that she's gotten for herself from me." She picked up the phone and had to wait while her sister talked to someone else. Wanting to hang up, she knew that she'd only call back and she'd not be happy with her. Suddenly she was talking to her.

"I got me the most amazing gift from you." All she said was no. "Don't be like that. You don't even know what it is."

"I've told you this before, Justine. I'm not going to be buying you gifts for your birthday anymore that I didn't pick out on my own." She said that she doesn't get her what she wants. "I can't afford what you want. And you're nearly forty years old. You're a little old to be hoping for a gift from your little sister."

"Why do you have to be like that? Bringing up my age two days before my birthday." She said that her birthday was in two weeks. "So. I should have a month to celebrate my birthday. It's not every day that someone turns forty, as you might know."

"I don't care. I'm not going to foot the price of whatever you think that I'm going to be paying for." She said that she'd already put down a deposit. "Get it back. I'm not going to be footing the bill for anything. I thought you would have learned your lesson last year and the years before. I'm not going to be paying for whatever you got yourself. That's final."

"You're so mean to me all the time, Sammy. I just don't understand you. I'll get my deposit back, but I'm not going to be happy with you for a year. You can bet you're not going to be getting anything from me either when your birthday comes around." She explained to her that she'd never gotten her anything for her birthday. "And this is why. You've managed to ruin my day with this. This trip would have been the trip of a lifetime."

"No." Justine simply hung up on her. Putting the handle back in the cradle, she was glad once again that she didn't have a cell phone that her sister knew about. If she had, she'd be calling her back in an hour and telling her something else that she'd gotten for her gift from her, and they'd have to start all over again with her telling her no.

She used to have a great deal of trouble telling her sister no. There was a time when she'd go into debt just to pay for whatever she got for herself that she expected her to pay for. Then she'd smartened up. Or nearly became homeless. That was a feeling that she never was having again, to not just be out of work but out of money for even crackers and cheese to eat.

"Did she hit you up?" She told Donald that she'd not been able to tell her what it was, but she was mad. "Good for you. I knew you were smarter than you looked, and you know that I think you're about as ugly as they come."

"Thanks. You date much with that sort of charm?" Donald had been saying the same thing to her since she'd hired him to work in her little restaurant. It had been about the time she'd learned to tell her sister no and to have won one of the largest lotteries that had ever been established. Those three things changed her life for the better, and she had never looked back.

Going back to her office, she finished up with the

order she put in and finished up the schedule that was for the next month. She could do that now that she had established a good working place for people to come to work. Sammy made a habit of hiring people who had only just gotten out of prison for various crimes, mostly white collar. And having a good working environment.

She wouldn't hire abusers, nor would she hire anyone who harmed children. She would run very extensive background checks on everyone, and when it came back with just a hint of abuse on it, she wouldn't hire them. She'd grown up in that kind of setting, and she wasn't going to let anyone in that had hit people.

That's why she didn't understand her sister. Justine had suffered as much as she had at the hands of their parents. More so since she was older. But on a daily basis, they would either be beaten, starved, or both. It was as if their lives were so unimportant to their parents that they could and would forget about them for days on end. Then, when they remembered them, it would be days of daily abuse and starvation, along with mental abuse that nearly destroyed her older sister.

It had taken Justine several years before she'd go out of the house. She was terrified that their parents were going to find them and hurt them. She didn't know what she'd done, but after going to visit her once, she'd not only come out of her home, but she began socializing with others too. It was such a transformation that she still, to this day, was waiting for her to have a breakdown and do something dangerous to herself.

Once she finished up for the day, she sat in her office and enjoyed her drink. It wasn't often that she'd have ten minutes to herself, and she was going to take advantage of it. As she was leaning back in her chair, her office phone rang. It couldn't be her sister, she didn't have this number as it was private and no one had it.

"My name is Storm Walsh, and I was wondering if I could have a word with you." She asked her how she got the number. "You know it, so I was able to get it. It wasn't as easy as I thought. You have a very complex mind."

"I don't know what that means, so I'm going to assume that you haven't complimented me. What do you want?" The woman laughed, and she felt her temper flare up. "I'm having my first break since I got out of bed this morning, and you're fucking it up. What do you want and just so you know, the answer is going to be no. I have no trouble saying that nowadays."

"No, I was just speaking to your sister, and she is upset with you—"

"What do you mean you were just speaking to my sister. Justine has her own life, and if she said I was going to pay for something, she'd be wrong about that, too. So whatever you're selling, I don't want it. Neither does she." The laughter again, and this time, she found herself smiling. It was the sound of bells. She hadn't any idea why it made her smile, but she did, and it lessened her temper just enough that she could talk to the woman. "Look. Justine has it in her head that I have an endless supply of money. I don't. I have investments as well as other things that my money is going for. Whatever she conned you into, I have nothing to do with it."

"She doesn't know you won the lottery, does she? In fact, no one knows that you won nor that you're the only one that did that week." She asked her how she'd found out. "I told you, when you know something, I can find it. Not as easy as I thought it would be, but it's right there in your mind for me to pick through."

"You've read my mind. I didn't get that the first time you said it. What is it you want? I'm not going to get suckered into a blackmail scheme with you. Whatever you think you know, it's not going to get me to pay you hundreds of thousands of dollars, so you don't tell on me. So state your business, and let me tell you no as well, and we'll end this conversation right now." She told her that she didn't need her money. "That's what everyone says just before they tell you how much they want from you."

"All right, I'm going to get to the point. Several days ago, there was a man that came into your offices to get on as a potential job. And in doing so, you were going to do a background check on him. That would have led you straight to me. But he got waylaid and didn't get to see you, so we have to do this the old-fashioned way. I call you. Now. I don't know what was supposed to happen when you hired him. Once he got to your office and met you, you were to go to me, and since that didn't happen for either of us, you didn't get to meet my son, Melbourne. He's your mate." She didn't say anything, thinking that the woman was quite mad. "I'm not mad at all but a very brilliant woman. I will tell anyone that. But you and Melbourne were to meet, and it didn't happen, and it has to."

"Perhaps the fates decided that I wasn't supposed to meet him after all. Maybe they realized their mistake and decided to waylay him, and they were finished with me and him." Storm said it didn't work that way and that she was indeed supposed to meet him. "Whatever the reason that I didn't, I'm happy for that. I don't want to meet anyone who thinks that I'm going to be their slave forever."

"Why does everyone think that? Has everyone read the same book and come to the conclusion that you have to be a slave to a shifter? I don't know, but

I do know that it won't work that way with him. He's a good man, and you two will have a good long life together. I promise you I raised him better than that." Sammy told her good for her. "Yes, and it will be good for you as well. You must meet him."

"No thanks. See how that worked? I told you that I'm really good at saying no. I have things in my life just the way that I want them, and I don't want a man in my life. I had one of those in my father, and I don't want to go through that again. You have a nice day, Storm, and I hope you find someone to pawn your son off on. It's not going to be me."

Hanging up the phone, she felt really good about herself. But her break time was over now, and she had things to do. When her phone rang again, she stepped out of the office and went about her daily chores at the restaurant. There were a million and one reasons she didn't want to talk to Storm again, and only one of them had to do with her supposed son, who was to be her mate.

Before You Go...

HELP AN AUTHOR
write a review
THANK YOU!

Share your voice and help guide other readers to these wonderful books. Even if it's only a line or two, your reviews help readers discover the author's books so they can continue creating stories that you'll love. Log in to your favorite retailer and leave a review. Thank you.

AWARD WINNING, BESTSELLING AUTHOR

Kathi Barton, a winner of the Pinnacle Book Achievement Award and a best-selling author on Amazon and All Romance books, lives in Nashport, Ohio, with her husband, Paul. When not creating new worlds and romance, Kathi and her husband enjoy camping and going to auctions. She can also be seen at county fairs with her husband, an artist and potter.

Her muse, a cross between Jimmy Stewart and Hugh Jackman, brings her stories to life for her readers in a way that has them coming back time and again for more. Her favorite genre is paranormal romance, with a great deal of spice. You can visit Kathi online and drop her an email if you'd like. She loves hearing from her fans. aaronskiss@gmail.com.

Follow Kathi on her blog: http://kathisbartonauthor.blogspot.com/

www.ingramcontent.com/pod-product-compliance
Lightning Source LLC
Chambersburg PA
CBHW020752210626
46807CB00018B/2527